D0722876

This book is a work of fiction. All characters, names, locations, and events portrayed in this book are fictional or used in an imaginary manner to entertain, and any resemblance to any real people, situations, or incidents is purely coincidental.

RETURNING MY SISTER'S FACE
And Other Far Eastern Tales of Whimsy and Malice

Eugie Foster

Copyright © 2009 by Eugie Foster

Introduction Copyright © 2009 by Vonda N. McIntyre

All Rights Reserved.

Cover Art:
"Kitsune," Copyright © 2009 by Ahyicodae

Cover Design Copyright © 2009 by Vera Nazarian

ISBN-13: 978-1-60762-010-5
ISBN-10: 1-60762-010-3

FIRST EDITION
Trade Hardcover

March 1, 2009

A Publication of
Norilana Books
P. O. Box 2188
Winnetka, CA 91396
www.norilana.com

Printed in the United States of America

Returning My Sister's Face

And Other Far Eastern Tales of Whimsy and Malice

Norilana Books

Fantasy

www.norilana.com

Foster, Eugie.
Returning my sister's
face : and other Far Eas
2009.
33305216935225
mi   04/10/09

Returning My Sister's Face

And Other Far Eastern Tales
of Whimsy and Malice

Eugie Foster

Introduction
by
Vonda N. McIntyre

For Matthew, who feeds my whimsy and acknowledges my malice, and who still loves me anyway.

Contents:

Eugie Foster in Many Dimensions

by Vonda N. McIntyre

In *Returning My Sister's Face and Other Far Eastern Tales of Whimsy and Malice,* Eugie Foster shares with her readers an exploration of her roots as a first-generation Chinese-American, and her interest in folk and fairy tales of many cultures.

The retellings of Chinese and Japanese folk tales, deeply romantic and highly stylized, sing with the truth of the real world and human and animal relationships. An-ying the heroic fire rabbit, magically changed, puzzles out human society (focused on and commanded by the male of the species, how strange to a rabbit!) and its inconstant love. Reading her story, both triumph and tragedy, I completely believed in the magical rabbit; and everyone should have a grandmother like Nai-nai: "Must destiny always knock so loudly?"

Her stories range from the light-hearted "The Tanuki-Kettle," introducing readers not familiar with Japanese mythology (or Miyazaki films) to the charming trickster raccoon dog, cousin to Coyote; through the utterly romantic "The Tiger Fortune Princess," to the creepily sinister "Returning My Sister's

Face," in which Happily Ever After lasts an all too short length of time. A number of her stories extend past the love-at-first-sight, happily-ever-after moments of Western fairy tales and explore the more complicated realms of suspicion, deception, and betrayal.

I met Eugie Foster at the Launchpad Astronomy Workshop, astronomer and sf writer Mike Brotherton's gathering for writers who want to get the science right in their fiction. It was Astronomy 101 in a week, with bells and whistles. Great fun, and our brains were full when the week ended. Eugie was the first of us to come up with an idea for a book springing directly from the course material. I hope some smart publisher snaps it up, because I think it would be terrific and I know a lot of kids I'd like to give it to for the winter holiday of their choice. (My block alone is home to a soccer team's worth of little girls.)

Eugie's biography always mention her pet skunk and her interest in folk tales; I'll add her quick mind and sense of humor and her ability to look well put-together at what for most writers qualifies as 0-dark-o'clock, not to mention the talent to conceive, write, and pull off a story with the title "My Friend is a Lesbian Zombie" (stay tuned for the next collection!).

Vonda N. McIntyre
October 2008

Daughter of Bótù

Buddha teaches that this existence is one of suffering. And of all the Middle Kingdom, my people, the Clan of Bótù, bear the greatest burden of suffering. We are fodder for all—tiger and owl, fox and man—and only those with fleet limbs, strong hearts, and good fortune survive.

But Buddha also teaches that it is desire which causes suffering, and if we follow the Eightfold Path, we will know enlightenment and immortality, and our suffering will end. Thus, my people look to Bótù, the immortal Jade Rabbit, to hearten us with his example, and we pray to his moon shadow for strength.

This I meditated upon as I nibbled my sparse meal of centipede grass. My mouth complained that the fibrous stalks were tasteless and parched, but I ignored it and advised my grumbling belly to rejoice, for it was fortunate to have even this. My admonishments failed to persuade my belly, especially when I did not consume every last blade, but at least its protestations lessened. I gathered the final stalks together and carried them away.

Beneath the earth, in the echoing corridors of our *louju*, Mama crouched in the den we shared. She was still beautiful—

the graceful arch of her paws, her long ears a study in elegance, and the perfect moon-roundness of her face—though grief and hunger had dried her coat to a brittle mat. Eyes closed, she might have been asleep but for the flicker of her nose.

"Mama, I brought you some centipede grass. I can't recommend its taste, but it's an improvement upon nothing."

Her whiskers trembled, but otherwise, it was as though I wasn't there. I crept to her side, offering what warmth and comfort I could.

"Won't you try some, Mama? It's better than the sedge grass we had two nights ago."

Nai-nai stood at the den's entrance. "Aiyah. All you could find was centipede grass, An-ying?" I hadn't heard her behind me, but Nai-nai had an uncanny aptitude for treading silently; it was probably why she'd lived so long.

"I'm afraid so," I replied, "and not very much of it, for all the distance I foraged to find it. Has Mama not stirred since I left?"

Nai-nai's ragged ears drooped, and she shook her head. She came over to sniff the centipede grass. "Have a mouthful," she coaxed, nudging Mama with her nose.

Mama's soft ears flicked at Nai-nai's words, but she made no move to sample the grass.

Nai-nai and I exchanged worried nose touches.

"An-ying, come with me," she said. "I think a little bark has grown on the willow tree by the ravine."

Obediently, I lollopped after her, although I knew we had already gnawed the willow bare.

An eeriness followed Nai-nai through our forsaken *louju*, with her paws soundless as nightfall. Like chasing a spirit guide in the underworld. Once, these tunnels had abounded with the prosperous bustle of my tribe. But a spate of bad fortune—an epidemic of the panting disease, a murderous band of foxes, and this endless drought—had sent many upon the path to their next lives. Those who remained had pronounced this *louju* cursed and abandoned it, seeking better fortune elsewhere.

I'd stayed because Mama would not leave. And Nai-nai was too old to travel, so she said. Three *ci* rabbits of the clan sharing a *louju* with death.

When we reached the south entrance, Nai-nai stopped.

"An-ying, there is great passion in you," she said. "A blessing and a curse, I have always maintained, you having been born in both the year and the hour of the rabbit but also beneath the auspice of fire. Fire rabbits are impetuous and brash."

"But I—"

She bumped me with her shoulder. "Outspoken and discourteous, too."

"I'm sorry, Nai-nai." I lowered my head and flattened my ears in a conciliatory manner.

She nibbled my fur. "I'm not angry, granddaughter, but you should know we feared for you, your mother and I. Even your coat is marked by fire, and it is well known that fire rabbits die young."

I glanced at the plume of red-gold fur that blossomed across my side like a tongue of fire.

"It is why I named you '*An*,' to balance the fire with calmness. But your mother—" Nai-nai twitched a whisker in annoyance. "—aiyah, water rabbits are such romantics, your mother insisted your name reflect her wishes for you, and so she named you '*ying*,' beauty. And you have at least fulfilled that aspect of your name."

I snuffled modestly.

"But now it is neither tranquility nor beauty which you must draw to you, but fire. A water rabbit will not withstand this drought, and even an old earth rabbit like your nai-nai will wither before much longer. Then what will you do? A young *ci* by yourself with no *xióng* to marry, no one to help you raise kits. And what if the rains never come? It's only luck that has kept us from starvation until now. Even fire, eventually, runs out of fuel to burn."

"What are you saying?"

"I have consulted your horoscope, An-ying, and your destiny is clear. You must leave the *louju*. Your mother and I are no longer young, and our departure from this realm is of no great consequence. But you—"

I shivered. Abandon my home and desert my family? "I can't leave Mama and you to die."

"There is no other way. It is your destiny."

"Destiny or no, I will find a way to save you." I pushed past her and bolted into the purple blanket of night. I ran, not caring where my paws took me, until my breath tore my throat and my heart was a frenzied dance.

Panting, I slowed to a lope and stopped. I stood upon the crest of an arid hill. The sparse grass and shrubs dotting the slope were scorched husks, desolate and inedible. Overhead, the moon was a fat, silver boat floating serenely upon a black river.

I raised my nose to the sky and contemplated Bótù's silhouette. "O honorable and glorious Immortal Rabbit, I know I have often strayed from the Eightfold Path, but my intentions have always been good. Please, I must believe that there is another destiny for me than to forsake Mama and Nai-nai to starvation. But I'm only a humble *cí*, and I despair that I'm too ignorant to perceive it. You teach us that the path to enlightenment is sacrifice, so I give myself to your will. Tell me to throw myself to a tiger or offer myself to a hawk, and I will do it, if only it will bring the rain. Venerable Bótù, I beg you, hear your daughter's prayer."

When I finished, the moon turned away from me. I trembled. Had I been too bold? Had I offended the Jade Rabbit?

The sky grumbled, and I realized why the moon had darkened. Storm clouds unfurled in a widening veil across the sky, obscuring the white face. Rejoicing, I pricked my ears, hoping for another rumble of thunder.

Instead, I heard something else—the beat-beat of danger, the drumbeat of strong, hind legs on the Earth's parched back.

Who struck it? It didn't matter. Both warning and command, it goaded my heart. *Match me, beat-beat, match me. Run!*

I ran.

All else fell from me—hunger, grief, hope—and my mind emptied, for to corrupt the heart with fear is death when the earth-drum fills it. I became flying hind legs, the breath of night through my fur, and my surging heart.

The sky fractured in a deafening crash; water poured down. And there was chaos.

I burst upon a nightmare scene of fearsome monsters and splintered shadows. The stink of predator, fox-wolf-tiger, assailed my nose. A demon limned in lightning turned its long face to me. Four pillars slammed down, miraculously missing me. Violence rang in my ears; sounds distorted by the rain.

I threw myself across their path, straining to outrace the wind. I did not feel teeth in my back, claws tearing my side. I was not relieved or thankful, too single-minded for such luxuries. I ran.

I leaped for the sanctuary of dry hedge and prickly bush. Concealment exacted a toll of rent fur, a price I paid willingly.

I sped to the familiar landscape of our *louju* and skittered to a stop. Three massive juniper trees had sprung, full-grown, atop the mounded earth which should have been our roof. They leaned, one upon another, their entwined arms a sweeping vault overhead. A human dwelling nestled between them, its rigid walls flowing like water from trunk to trunk. How could it, they, be here? And where were Mama and Nai-nai?

The panic I'd left behind, that I had outrun, caught me. My heart, filled with earth-drum and now terror, failed.

I had time to wonder whether Mama and Nai-nai had escaped before the tree roots had crushed our *louju*. Then I had no more thoughts.

"Aiyah, you will be soaked through! An-ying, come in out of the rain."

I stirred, disoriented. "Nai-nai, did you and Mama make it outside?"

"Foolish girl, it is not we who must go outside, but you who must come in. Get up. Or must I drag my old bones into the rain to fetch you?"

I opened my eyes and another shock struck my heart. Nai-nai had become a—a human! She stood in the doorway of the dwelling, scowling, arms crossed. Her body was swathed in yellow and saffron silk that shimmered like sunlight skipping over a pond. A sash wrapped her waist, embroidered with flowers and dates. Her face was naked brownness, clad with creases instead of fur. But despite the strange form she wore, I knew it was Nai-nai.

She raised her arm to beckon me, as comfortable in her new shape as she'd been in her old.

I scrambled up, amazed to find myself also wearing a human body. My arms were weighted by silk the color of dawn, so at first I could not find my paws. Or *hands*, rather. A billow of vermilion tangled my legs, fastened by a red-gold sash that dangled to the ground. A tightness about my head was an elaborate arrangement of ridiculously lengthy fur bristling with what felt like rocks and sticks—which succeeded, briefly, in distracting me from the travesty my lovely ears had become. They were stumps! Tiny and useless, I couldn't even twitch them. And the final wonder, human speech, with all its unrabbity terms and notions, filled my head.

Unlike Nai-nai, I was ill at ease. In the handful of steps to the door I stumbled twice, entangled in folds of silk. Finally, Nai-nai hobbled out, complaining of the rain. Although in truth, the juniper canopy protected us from all but the most determined raindrops.

"I'm a human, Nai-nai," I wailed.

"Yes, I know," she said, utterly matter-of-fact.

"So are you!"

She half-dragged, half-led me inside. "And before you amaze me with another revelation, your mother is as well."

"But, how?"

Nai-nai closed the door behind us. "We are Daughters of Bótù," she said, as though that explained everything. At my uncomprehending look, she scowled, "We three are directly descended from the Jade Rabbit. It is a legacy which prompts the cosmos to favor us with human forms. I think it no favor at all but a bother. Humankind is wicked and corrupt, and I have little use for this shape. However, destiny is destiny. No one ever consults me about it."

Inside, the house was simple but elegant, with a cozy sitting room containing furnishings of carved rosewood and teak. A straw mat cushioned the floor, and decorated screens concealed corridors and windows. Quite sizable, like our *louju*, it was meant for more than three.

Mama looked up from where she reclined on a low chair by a crackling fire. She wore a garment that wrapped her arms in the paleness before a storm and her legs in the deep indigo of twilight in summer. Her hair was piled upon her head like a cloud. Blue agate combs dangled with ornaments depicting the three phases of the moon: slender crescent, full face, and waning gibbous.

She was as beautiful a human as she had been a rabbit. I moved towards her and tripped over my hem.

"I can't walk in this," I exclaimed, kicking and floundering on the floor in a welter of silk. "And I can't balance on these stubby feet. They're so tiny! Why aren't humans constantly toppling over?"

"Aiyah, I'm too old for this." Nai-nai pulled an oval fan from her sash and waved it. "Stop thinking of your *ruqun*, your garment, as separate from yourself. Why are you not always bumbling over your trailing ears or sent sprawling by your large rabbit feet?"

"Because they are me," I retorted, "and only newborn kits cannot get their bodies aligned with their wills."

"Well, kit, your *ruqun* is as much you as your pelt was. When we transformed, all that we were became as we now are. So stop thinking of your body and garments as something to vie against."

Dubious, I did as Nai-nai advised and ceased trying to guide leg and arm, but merely thought "stand" and "walk." To my surprise, I managed to cross the room without losing my balance or becoming snarled in my skirt.

I kneeled by Mama. "Mama, how are you?"

Her eyes passed over me, and she turned to the fire.

I sagged, disappointed. What good was a new shape if every wound upon our souls remained? My broodings were interrupted by thumpings at the door.

"Hello, you inside!" The voice was a man's, crackling with worry. "My master is hurt, and we are lost. I beg you, give us shelter from the rain."

"Must destiny always knock so loudly?" Nai-nai shuffled to the door.

Trailing after, I peeked from behind her.

Outside, a slender young man garbed in a torn tunic of white hemp bowed low. "Honored grandmother," he said. "I am Guan Shi, humble companion and guard to the illustrious Bei Huangong." He indicated the man leaning heavily upon our doorframe. Bei Huangong had a ragged band of cloth knotted around his head. His face was pale over the ginger of his cross-collar shirt and damson overcoat. A growing splotch of wetness darkened the bandage.

With a start, I recognized them. They were the monsters that had so frightened me earlier as I blundered into their midst. Not demons, but only a hunting party and their horses.

"Well, don't just stand dripping on our threshold," Nai-nai said, unimpressed by the formal introduction. "Come in. We don't have a stable, but you may tie your mounts to the trees."

Guan Shi bowed again until I thought he must be kin to a squirrel, forever bobbing its head about. "We are honored by your generous hospitality."

With Guan Shi's assistance, Bei Huangong drooped gratefully to our couch.

"An-ying, heat some water," Nai-nai commanded. "And fetch my white pouch."

It was like remembering a dream. I knew what to do, although I did not know how I could. I lifted the iron pot from its hook and set it over the flames. Then I hurried to Nai-nai's den, demarked by a yellow screen with a prancing *qilin* painted upon it. Her pouch, a lumpy bag large enough to contain a piglet, lay beside her bed. Touching it gave me a momentary shock, rabbit fur without the rabbit.

I hastened to bring it to her, and Nai-nai dumped medicines and ointments from its depths.

"Let us see how destiny has treated you," she said and began unwrapping the bandage from Bei Huangong's temple.

"What happened?" I asked Guan Shi.

He bowed, and I had the urge to push him back upright. "A miracle, most certainly, honorable lady. My master was pursuing a demon hind, although we didn't know it was a demon at the time. We rode so far and fast after her, we lost our way. The rainstorm broke, half-blinding us, as she bounded over a thicket wall. My master spurred his horse to follow, but then a crimson rabbit sprang out, as though conjured from the air, and flung itself across my master's path."

I gasped, for of course I recognized myself. Although, admittedly, "crimson" seemed a bit overstated.

"My master's horse reared," Guan Shi's continued, "throwing him, and he cracked his head on a tree. I cursed the rabbit then, what a fool I was. It had saved his life! You see, I happened to glance over the thicket my master had been preparing to leap. It opened upon tragedy, a drop-off lined with jagged rocks at the bottom. No man could have survived such a fall. Of the hind, there was no sign. A thousand blessings upon that rabbit. Surely it was a good spirit."

"A spirit?" Nai-nai snorted. "More likely a frightened rabbit scampering willy-nilly about."

A faint voice joined our discussion. "I do not possess your bounty of wisdom, grandmother, but I'm certain it was a spirit." Despite Bei Huangong's weakness, his voice carried authority, the assurance of one accustomed to obedience.

"I suppose it told you that after you knocked your head?" Nai-nai asked.

He chuckled. "No, but it would've been worth the bump if it had. After my fall, I was too dizzy to ride, and we were utterly lost. But the rabbit spirit saved us again. It marked the direction we should take with its own red fur and guided us to the tendril of smoke from your fire."

"It did, did it?" Nai-nai pinioned me with an arch glare. "How fortunate indeed." She administered a damp plaster to Bei Huangong's head. "The cut isn't deep, but the fall has rattled your skull. You'll wait several days to ride or travel if you care about what's good for you. Also, you mustn't sleep tonight, or you might not wake tomorrow. Best if someone keeps you company."

"I'll gladly stay up with my master," Guan Shi said.

Nai-nai eyed him. "You are swaying on your feet. You would doze off within the hour."

"I wouldn't—"

"No, you rest in there." She nodded at a screen painted with cranes.

Bei Huangong waved his hand, silencing any further protest, although lines furrowed the space between Guan Shi's eyes.

"Don't fret," Nai-nai said. "I'll brew some medicine, and An-ying will make sure your lord doesn't drowse."

Bei Huangong smiled at me. "I'm surely blessed by the spirits. They save my life, guide us here, and now I am to have a beautiful nurse to converse with for the whole night."

I lowered my eyes, suddenly shy. I hadn't thought to become accustomed to human faces so easily. But the smoothness of Bei Huangong's brow, the way his mouth quirked when he spoke, I found these natural, appealing even, not caring that he had no fur or such tiny ears.

Nai-nai snorted. "An-ying, if your eyelids start to droop, you'll give that Guan Shi a shake and get him up, yes?"

"Yes, Nai-nai."

She sprinkled some herbs into the iron pot. "Let that steep. Give him a cup when the water is the same color as spring moss, and another two swallows every half hour." She waved her finger at him. "You drink it all, you hear?"

"Yes, grandmother." Bei Huangong inclined his head but then winced. "I would swallow mud if it relieved this troublesome hammering."

"Good. Now, my bones are old, and this night has been long. I'm off to sleep." She shuffled away to the yellow-screened room, shooing Guan Shi before her.

Still bashful, I poured a cup of the moss-green tea for Bei Huangong.

He grimaced at the taste. "Why must medicine always be bitter?"

"I suppose to encourage us to take greater care so we will not require it."

"Now that's a sensible answer. Much better than the ramblings of my physicians."

My face grew warm, and my breath quickened as though I bounded full speed down a hill.

"Why, I believe your grandmother's brew has quelled the hammering. So, what shall we talk about?" He beckoned to Mama in her chair by the fire. "I don't mean to exclude you, madam. Shall we all play a word game?"

Mama shook her head. She rose and drifted to a rain-colored screen with a black tortoise swimming across it. With a fluid bow, she disappeared behind it.

"I didn't mean to offend," Bei Huangong said.

"It wasn't you. Mama doesn't talk. Ever since a fox stole my baby brother, she hasn't spoken."

"A fox?"

"We found my brother on our doorstep, ringed by fox prints, his throat ripped out. The fox did it for sport, you see, not hunger. Nai-nai says Mama's voice followed my brother's soul to the underworld of Huang-chuan so that she may comfort him with lullabies. I think a portion of her soul followed him too."

Bei Huangong's eyes darkened. "How terrible. Double tragedy to lose a family member to a fox and also one so young. And you three ladies live alone? Where's your father?"

"He became ill and died not long after the fox took my brother."

"So much tragedy for one so lovely."

"Buddha teaches that this existence is one of suffering." I studied my white hands with their peculiar and useful side digit. "I try to rejoice that my loved ones suffer no more."

"My priests would applaud your devout and philosophic outlook."

I tried to smile, but couldn't. "Don't be deceived. I'm a poor philosopher. Truthfully, I cannot stop myself from missing them."

"It's natural to grieve. I, too, have experienced a loss." He covered my hand with his. "Sometimes, there is no solace to be found."

Where his hand touched mine, I prickled with awareness, sensitive to his radiant warmth, the thrill of skin on skin, the cool caress of silk. Was this why humans covered themselves, because lacking fur, they were susceptible to such distracting and delicious sensations?

"Who–who do you grieve for?" I asked.

"My father died last year. A hunting accident." He sighed and slipped his hand away, and I regretted my question. "My stepmother blames me that I wasn't the one leading the hunt that day. In a fashion, it's because of her I was out this night. Our food stores have dwindled from this drought, and she lamented to me that the remaining meat in our larder was gamy. I hoped that an offering of fresh venison would soften her, a little, maybe. You can imagine how overjoyed I was to glimpse that hind and how eager I was to acquire her. But it was only the mockery of demons." He touched the poultice on his head. "I admit, I'm a poor philosopher, too. There are times when I wish it had been me instead of my father on that terrible hunt. I despair that I'll never be the lord he was."

"Don't say such things." I took Bei Huangong's hand back and laced my fingers through his. "Nai-nai says that each of us has a destiny, one that cannot be escaped, and to rail at destiny is the province of madmen and fools."

He regarded my hand with surprise, although he didn't pull away. Had I behaved inappropriately? But surely, he had done it first.

"Lady An-ying, I had not properly considered our situation before. Perhaps you would prefer that Guan Shi sleep on the floor out here by the fire?"

"What? Why would I want that? The poor thing would wake with a terrible bend in his neck."

"Otherwise, we have no chaperone to safeguard your honor."

I laughed. "Are you saying I should fear for my honor with you?"

His eyes sparkled. "As lovely as you are, I think I can manage to maintain a proper decorum. It's your reputation I am considering. Are you not concerned about flapping tongues?"

"Who is there to gossip to out here? The insects and birds care little about our doings."

"I see. So—" He pulled me closer until I could feel his breath on my face. "If I were to, say, steal a kiss, there would be no harm?"

I could have broken free. Not only because he was hurt and weak, but also, there was no coercion in his touch. To keep me there required my consent.

"There's no need to steal something freely given." I closed the space between us.

Bei Huangong tasted of heat and smoke, strong wind and salt. The fire in me approved, and I wanted the kiss to never stop. It was Bei Huangong who broke from it, wincing.

"Forgive me, but that irksome hammering has resumed."

"Oh, I forgot your medicine!" I rushed off to measure two swallows of Nai-nai's tea.

I would not have slept that night even if Bótù had flown down from the moon and commanded me to. Bei Huangong taught me how to play Go using crumbled bits of charcoal from the fire and leftover scraps of Guan Shi's undershirt—the origin of the makeshift bandage—as pieces and the straw mat as a board. He told me of his palace, and I told him of the quiet peace of the forest. I worried that my prattle would bore him asleep, but he listened, rapt, to my poor efforts to describe the autumn trees at twilight, dripping gold and silver in the fading light.

Too soon, a blush of palest gold through painted screens announced the dawn, and shortly after, Nai-nai bustled in.

"Everyone still awake? Good, good."

Bei Huangong astonished me by heaving himself from the couch to kneel before her. "Grandmother, may I assume you are An-ying's guardian?"

Nai-nai frowned. "As much as she needs a guardian, I suppose."

He swayed, his face losing some of the color it had gained in the night, and Nai-nai stuck a gnarled hand out to steady him.

"You should lie down. You're still sick."

He continued, undeterred. "I'm a respected nobleman, kin to the emperor. I can provide references, if you like."

Nai-nai eyed me over Bei Huangong's head. "An-ying,

what's all this about?"

I spread my hands, as baffled as she.

"Grandmother, may I have your blessing to petition An-ying's affections?" Bei Huangong blurted. "I wish to court her."

"Ah, I see." Nai-nai's mouth puckered. "I'd hoped she would take up with one of our clan, but no one cares about my opinion. Do as you like. I'm not foolish enough to meddle in her destiny, anyway."

He took this as assent, and I remained bemused at the strangeness of human ways.

How to describe our courtship? I forgot the meaning of time when I was with Bei Huangong. We were fire meeting fire, and it seemed nothing could extinguish our fervor, not even the incessant rains.

But as the moon burgeoned, so did Bei Huangong's strength. Standing no longer brought dizziness, and the hammering in his head departed for good. While I rejoiced at his health, nevertheless, every color became less vivid to me, a match to the sky's lusterless gray. A simple, pastoral life could never be the destiny of a man such as Bei Huangong. So I was prepared for heartbreak when he turned serious eyes to me as we strolled beneath dripping branches.

"An-ying, I must return home," he said.

"Yes." I didn't trust myself to say more.

"Come with me. Marry me."

With that question, color returned to my world.

Nai-nai glowered at Bei Huangong when he announced our betrothal. But it's not our way to deny love, and once I'd assured her that I wanted this more than soft fur and whiskers, the elusive perfume of earth and grass, and the ecstasy of bounding on strong rabbit legs beneath the night sky, her protests ended. Mama only gazed at me with distant eyes and kissed my cheek.

"Come with us," I begged them. "Bei Huangong says there's plenty of room—"

"No," Nai-nai said. "Your mother and I are acquainted with that world, and we don't wish to revisit it. And besides, I'm too old to travel."

"But how can I leave you?"

"Do not worry for us. Now that the rains have come, we'll be fine. I told you it was your destiny to leave us, didn't I?"

"Oh, Nai-nai—" The lines of her face blurred in an overflow of tears.

"Enough of that. Here." She pressed two items into my hands. One was a round mirror of white jade, the full moon framing the silvered glass. Three rabbits of inlaid mother-of-pearl adorned the back, their leaping bodies forming an everlasting circle. The other was a little sickle knife, the hilt a jade rabbit with ears streaming down its back. "There is great virtue in these talismans. They will remind you of who you are and who you are descended from."

When I looked into the mirror, reflected back was not the maiden An-ying, but the rabbit An-ying with whiskers and pink nose. But rabbit me wore dawn-colored silk, and a copper bird and a sprig of paper apricot blossoms—my hair ornaments—stuck out behind my long ears. It was a fanciful magic, unlike the more practical one which kept my *ruqun* fresh and pristine through mud and brambles.

I embraced her.

"Humph. Don't let Bei Huangong's world make you forget everything I've taught you."

Horseback riding was a new experience, one I didn't enjoy. The bouncing gait agitated my insides, and perching so high above the ground provoked a relentless apprehension. However, I did enjoy the way my lover clasped me so securely before him as we shared a saddle. And the strong legs of Bei Huangong and Guan Shi's steeds covered more terrain than I thought possible.

Bei Huangong's palace was enclosed by stone walls with round doorways and stylish, vase-shaped apertures. Brick-lined walkways meandered through a garden overflowing with climbing roses, camellias, and sweet osmanthus. Inside, the floors were a mosaic of vibrantly glazed tile, and a high, double-arched ceiling soared overhead. It was more beautiful than my most lavish imaginings.

In such idyllic surroundings, how could the flow of my destiny be anything but tranquil and harmonious? And yet, there was one eddy, Bei Huangong's stepmother.

Meng Shouzhen was an exquisite beauty, so glamorous, so elegant in her embroidered *shenyi*, her black hair glittering with jewels. The perfection of her plum-colored lips and willow leaf-shaped eyebrows overwhelmed me. And when I saw her eyes, I gaped like the ingénue I was. They were luminous, shining brighter than any of the gems in her hair, and most remarkable of all, they were golden.

"What a charming girl," she said, her voice as refined as the rest of her. "But then, I'm not that surprised. You would have to be extraordinary to have orchestrated such a prosperous match." She laughed, a scintillating ripple of sound. "You're a very fortunate girl indeed. Well, good for you. I cannot fault anyone for appreciating the finer things and wanting to better her character."

I bowed. "Th–thank you, madam. I've always striven to improve myself."

Bei Huangong stiffened as though I'd committed some grievous impropriety. But Meng Shouzhen only laughed more.

Later, I asked Bei Huangong to explain my blunder, and his lips tightened. "Never mind. Only try to watch what you say.

We're no longer in the forest, and my reputation as well as yours may be blackened by a thoughtless remark."

Distressed that my ignorance had caused him to lose face, I resolved to take greater care. But in no time at all, I bungled again. Bei Huangong surveyed me one morning, lines of displeasure crinkling his eyes.

"Must you always wear that *ruqun*?"

"Don't you like it?" I asked, astonished.

"It's fine, but you have closets brimming with rich silks and expensive brocades. Why not put on something different?"

"But I like my *ruqun*," I said. "Why do I need anything else?"

His mouth fell open then snapped shut. "Reluctant to flaunt new clothes? You are a most singular woman, An-ying. Nevertheless, while your unassuming sensibilities are laudable, people are talking. Li Fu said to me the other day, 'It's just as well your wife's so fond of that pink *ruqun*. What man's fortunes would be enough to maintain a second wardrobe the size of your stepmother's?'"

I blinked. "Who—?"

"It doesn't matter. My point is it's unbecoming for my bride to be seen so often in the same garment."

"I didn't realize. Of course I'll do as you suggest."

Initially, I pined for my *ruqun*, but it meant so much to Bei Huangong that I parade about in amber *zhaoshan* robes, peach *qun* skirts, burgundy *yi* jackets, and gauzy, sea green sashes. So I folded my *ruqun* away into a cedar chest, and after a while, the perpetual sense of having misplaced something lessened.

Our wedding was a sumptuous affair with towers of sophisticated dishes for me to sample. I regretted the disappointment in the head cook's face when I declined a serving of crackling duck as well as a slice of roast pork, but the thought of eating flesh curdled my stomach. At least his wounded expression changed to smiles when I praised his pan-fried dumplings and devoured two whole moon cakes, getting my hands sticky with sweet bean paste.

That night, Bei Huangong reverently divested me of my wedding *quju*, peeling away the heavy brocade embroidered with phoenixes as though I were a frail blossom that must be coaxed to bloom. In his arms, my qualms and uncertainties dissolved like sugar in the rain. If before we had been afire, now we rivaled the sun. For such bliss, I would withstand a hundred Meng Shouzhens, adorn myself in nettles, and learn to chirp like a cricket.

My status among Bei Huangong's people altered in small and peculiar ways. Men wouldn't exchange more than the most cursory of phrases with me, refusing to meet my eyes and grasping at the least excuse to escape my presence. Yet they scrutinized me so intently—from a safe distance—I feared I would leave a trail of calamities, such a distraction I posed. As for the women, they began to emulate me. If I wore lavender and topaz silk one day, the next it seemed I waded through a field of rustling lavender and topaz.

"It's most disconcerting," I commented to Guan Shi, as I waited for Bei Huangong to return from a meeting with some dignitaries. "Why do they do that?"

"They hope that by echoing you, some of your beauty will bounce onto them."

I giggled. "How foolish." I enjoyed Guan Shi's company. Not only because he was less a stranger, but he was perhaps the only man whose demeanor towards me hadn't changed. "Why, next to Meng Shouzhen, I'm as common and grubby as a mud-spattered stick. Why don't they imitate her?"

He bowed. "If you'll pardon my forthright words, it is inner beauty as well as outward appearance the court ladies admire. My master's stepmother possesses a fearsome beauty, but it is a splendor to quail before rather than to covet. While you are a delicate orchid, shy and winsome. Such beauty even a blind man would appreciate."

I was taken aback, both at his oblique criticism of Meng Shouzhen as well as of his appraisal of me. But Bei Huangong's arrival saved me from thinking of a response.

When he saw us, the corners of his mouth pulled down.

"What is it?" I asked. "What's the matter?"

"There's trouble to the south," he said. "Barbarian raiders. My borders are guarded by mountains and air, but less fortunate Hao Feigong wishes to drive them off before they ravage more than a few peasant villages. I am taking a garrison to join him in a concerted strike."

"You're leaving?"

"I must. Otherwise, I lose face with Hao Feigong." He raised a hand to cup my chin. "Don't look so bleak. If the rains persist, we may flood them out, and I'll be back before the osmanthus blossoms fade."

"Then I'll pray every day for rain."

The next morning he rode away at the head of a multitude of soldiers bristling with spears and bows, taking Guan Shi with him so I had no one at all to talk to. I'm ashamed to admit that as soon as the clatter of their departure faded, I hid myself away, even taking my meals in solitude. While I didn't concur with Guan Shi's assessment of "delicate orchid," "shy" was accurate. The scrutiny of my husband's people flustered me—what I wore, what I said, how I behaved—and I did not fully understand the standards by which they judged me. Without Bei Huangong to bolster my nerve, I preferred cheerless isolation.

Lacking the impetus of agenda or husband to accommodate, I reverted from a daylight routine to the nighttime habits of a rabbit. I explored the garden by starshine, nibbling the occasional rose petal or violet with delight, meditated upon Bótù's shadow as the moon wheeled across the sky, and admired my reflection in the moon mirror. Vanity notwithstanding, the soft-furred visage in the glass comforted me, made me feel less alone.

One drizzly evening, a wondrous revelation bolstered my spirits and made the hours less weighty. I determined that the swelling of my belly was not due to an overindulgence of rich food but budding new life. Although I became even more impatient for Bei Huangong's return, my nights passed in glorious musings. What would the baby be like? Would our child possess Bei Huangong's expressive eyes? Be clever like Nai-nai? Or beautiful like Mama? And how would the child's rabbit heritage manifest?

On a rain-filled day at the end of a rain-filled week, I awakened to an excited ruckus. Banners and horses had been sighted. Bei Huangong was coming home!

I dressed in awkward haste and rushed to greet him, arriving as my husband rode through the palace gates, mud-spattered and weary, but also triumphant.

"We executed a well-devised plan with prodigious results," he declared to the cheering throng. "Lured them to a drained gorge and released the river upon them. Swept those barbarians back to hell."

When his eyes lit upon me, they filled with joy, and I sped to his side. But then they darkened, and I slowed my steps, suddenly timid. It had been a long while since I'd been among so many people.

"Welcome home, my husband." I moved to embrace him, but he raised a hand.

"I'm caked in muck and dirt from the road."

"It doesn't bother me."

"Still, perhaps you would be so gracious as to allow me time to see to my men and cleanse away the mud. I'd be obliged if you could wait for me in our chambers."

"Oh, but—"

"An-ying, please do as I ask."

Crestfallen, I took myself away. But I soon cheered up. The dictates of human society were complex and baffling. I'd undoubtedly violated some silly custom involving muddy receptions. But soon we would share in the joyous anticipation of our child's birth.

The moon had risen before I heard his footsteps. As soon as he strode in, I ran to press his hand through azure silk to my distended belly.

"Bei Huangong, isn't it wonderful?" I babbled, too jubilant for restraint. "I worried you wouldn't return before his birth. It will be a son, I'm sure of it. Feel how he leaps?"

But his reaction wasn't as I expected. He yanked his hand away.

I tried not to look as hurt as I felt. "I thought you'd be pleased."

He studied me with haggard eyes. "I've tried to disregard Meng Shouzhen's insinuations, although it was difficult when you persisted in flirting with my servant."

"Flirting? You mean with Guan Shi? We only talked—"

"But now what am I to think?" He ignored my protests. "I come back to scandalized recriminations that you secluded yourself in my absence, only emerging at night like a thief. And now this. I had to endure pointing fingers and smirks behind my back the whole day. Not the homecoming I'd visualized, I assure you."

He'd never before spoken so harshly to me. "Bei Huangong—"

"I believed your eagerness in the forest was a testament of your love, that you never protested or pushed me away, leaving it to me to curb our ardor, out of innocence and trust."

"You wanted me to push you away?"

"In reality you must have been quite desperate to ensnare me. How you must have laughed at my credulity. But now the truth is out."

"I don't understand—"

He grabbed the borders of my *shan* and yanked the blue silk taut against my body. "This child comes too early to be mine! You hid it cunningly before, or perhaps I was too smitten to notice. But you've misplayed yourself. Sequestering yourself has only drawn attention to how gravid you are."

In a rush, I understood. "Oh, Bei Huangong, I should have told you before, but I thought—I thought, oh, I don't know what I thought."

"Told me what? That you are an opportunistic, scheming seductress?"

His words struck me like blades. "No! That I am a rabbit. Until the night you came to me, I ran on four paws and ate grass and slept in a den beneath the earth. It was I who ran across your path and startled your horse. It was my fur, torn by the brambles, which led you to our fire. I–I think it's because I'm a rabbit that our son quickens with such haste. Be assured, though, he is yours."

He stared at me for several, long heartbeats. "Well, that's inventive, at least. But I don't think it will mollify the people counting on their fingers. Or do you expect the baby to have two furred ears and gnaw on roots?" He thrust me away. "What fool do you take me for?"

I caught myself on the bed. "Why are you so determined to despise me?" I cried. "You condemn me without even the opportunity you allow a thief to prove his innocence. When our son is born, he will take after you and none other."

"Why wait until then?" he snapped. "Although from the look of you, I wouldn't be surprised if you dropped your brat tomorrow. I'll just ask the magistrate whether it's possible it could be mine, given that not three months have passed since the cursed day we met. It will be convenient. I'll present my question at the same time I petition him to divorce us."

"Divorce?" I gasped. "At least wait until he's born to see—"

"I suppose it would be uncivilized to dump you in the street as you are. But I'd be grateful if you took yourself to the outer courtyard. I don't want you polluting my chambers with your presence."

With those hateful words, he stormed out.

I burst into tears. Before I could compose myself or sort my thoughts, a trio of women arrived. They hefted my cedar chest and ushered it and me, still sobbing, to a mean little room with a slit for a window. Servant's quarters. For comfort, I had a single lantern and a straw mat on the floor.

I huddled on the thin mat, too stupefied to even light the lantern. The night passed in a haze of tears. Waking and sleeping were the same; I wept, eyes opened or closed, and dreamed of sorrow.

Morning arrived as jabbing fingers of sunlight through the window. My eyes were tear-crusted and hot, my face greasy with sweat, although I shivered in the dank air. I squinted, shielding my eyes with my hand, and saw I'd slept, after all. The window faced west; it was discourteous sunset that beset me, not the rudeness of dawn.

A needle of pain ran through me. Blue silk adhered to my skin as I heaved myself up and away from the noisome sun. Another pain followed the first—not a needle this time, but a nail—and I cried out.

The babe was coming, and I was alone.

In my anguish, I knew only desperation. Oh, Nai-nai, this is not how my son should arrive. You should be here to press your warm side against mine and to ease me with the birthing tales of our clan. My son should be born surrounded by the scent of soft fur and cool earth. I should have Mama's shoulder to rest my head on, her beautiful ears fluttering my whiskers like when I was a kit. Please help me, Nai-nai, Mama. I can't do this by myself.

The door swung open. Had my family miraculously heard my pleas and come? But the waning light revealed the last person I wanted or expected. Meng Shouzhen.

She spoke not one word of greeting, only crossed to the lantern and lit it. By its flame she stood, resplendent in a scarlet *shenyi*, and scrutinized me.

Another pain lanced through me, and I folded my body tight, fighting not to scream. It was an instinctive struggle, to suffer in silence and not invite a predator's interest.

As though I summoned peril with my thoughts, I scented fox. Delirium born of pain and sickness thickened the air with the stench of terror, violence, and death. I blinked my streaming eyes and gasped. Meng Shouzhen had transformed from a beautiful woman into a slavering vixen, yellow eyes aglow and sharp teeth glistening. The fox bent over me, its panting breath hot and fetid, eager to devour the newborn kit I labored to birth.

I screamed—foolish human response—and the vision cleared. But the fox scent hung in the air.

Meng Shouzhen tugged at my *shanqun*, loosening it and uncovering my legs. Her eyes glinted, the lantern's flame turning them molten and flat.

"You're a fox!" I blurted.

She smiled, baring pointed, white teeth. "Very true," she said. "Most perceptive of you, little rabbit."

My eyes widened.

"Oh, don't worry, your pretense is quite good. I'd never have guessed had not Bei Huangong confided in me. And you needn't look so stricken. He didn't know he was betraying you. He still has a bit of softness for you. Isn't that sweet? He begged me to tend you during your labor and told me how he feared you might be sick in the mind." She cackled, a terrible, barking call.

I froze. I must not move, must not stir so much as a whisker, and maybe the fox would overlook me.

"Don't worry, little rabbit, my teeth aren't for your throat, although I do owe you for your bothersome rescue. I'll content myself by killing your son. Can't have a little half-rabbit heir hopping about, not when I'm so close to inheriting it all."

Pain skewered me; I only shivered. But I couldn't stop the hot wetness that spilled from me, darkening the straw. My babe would die as soon as he was born. And I could do nothing, helpless as every mother is in the pangs of childbirth.

My body bowed, a gateway of agony, expelling my son into the world. He arrived in a rush of blood and despair. Meng Shouzhen took him before I even had the chance to hold him, severing the umbilical cord with her white teeth.

"No!" I struggled to raise myself, but she easily pushed me back.

She clasped him like a doll, untroubled by birth fluids upon her *shenyi*. Perhaps she'd worn scarlet to mask the blood.

"I'll tell Bei Huangong you're a fox," I panted. "Even if he doesn't believe me, a part of him will be vigilant."

"I do not think you will." She fixed me with burning, golden eyes, predator's eyes to paralyze a trembling rabbit. I couldn't blink, couldn't move, couldn't scream. Mesmerized by those flickering orbs, I was frozen, waiting for teeth to snap shut around my throat.

The mewling of a newborn rabbit called me back. No, not a rabbit, a human. My son. I roused, stumpy ears straining. All was silence. I was alone.

I dragged myself from the mat, shivering, aching, and weak. My fingers were half-numb stubs as I fumbled with the cedar chest's latch. I wrenched it open and pulled out my *ruqun*, wrapping it around me. My trembling lessened, and a thread of vigor warmed me. To think that once I'd railed against my *ruqun*. I knotted the red-gold sash, tucking the moon mirror and sickle knife into its folds.

Staggering from my exile, I scented fox in the corridor. Instinct clamored at me to turn tail; I didn't heed it. The fox-stink led me through the outer courtyard and into the palace, down jade-tiled walkways, until I came to the chambers I'd shared with Bei Huangong. Within, the curdling tang of blood masked the stench of fox.

A still shape lay on the bed, pale and silent. I knew what I'd find, but I crept there anyway.

He was so tiny, so helpless. His throat had been opened by razored teeth, and his blood had poured upon satin and silk. I lifted him, rocking him to my breast. I would have given him my voice, sung lullabies to him in Huang-chuan, but he'd never heard me sing, never heard me croon endearments. How would he know to be comforted?

Oh, my son, my kit! This existence is full of suffering. Let me rejoice that your time here was so brief.

We were interrupted by rushing feet. Meng Shouzhen hastened in with Bei Huangong behind her. They halted abruptly when they saw me, and I didn't wonder. I must have looked a sight, blood smearing my *ruqun* and my face twisted with grief.

"We're too late," Meng Shouzhen cried. "It's as I feared. Her madness has driven her to murder her own baby!"

I laid my son on the bed. His empty, lifeless body reminded me of another terrible night and another stolen child. In a burst of insight, I knew that the same fox who'd slaughtered my son had also killed my brother.

"I am not the murderess," I said, marveling at the calm of my voice. See, Nai-nai? You named me well, after all. "*You* murdered my son, Meng Shouzhen, as you intend to murder my husband, as you would have murdered him if I hadn't dashed across his path."

"Madwoman. She thinks she's a rabbit," Meng Shouzhen said.

I walked, slowly but steadily, to the pair by the door. "I *am* a rabbit, descended from Bótù." I pulled the moon mirror from my sash and turned its fanciful magic upon Meng Shouzhen. "Just as you are a fox, descended from malice."

Surprise, shock, and comprehension chased across Bei Huangong's face. I knew what he saw in the mirror: a fox in Meng Shouzhen's *shenyi*. He saw her as she was, scheming fox woman, bloodthirsty *huli jing*. The mirror revealed her true nature as surely as it did mine.

She knocked the mirror from my hand. "Preposterous," she snarled. "Some trick."

I caught a fold of her *shanyi* and drew the silver moon-knife. "Is this also a trick?" I slashed away a panel of scarlet silk.

She shrieked, and instead of a length of silk, I gripped a severed fox tail.

I hadn't fully understood what Nai-nai told me before, but I did now. We could take off our silks, fox and rabbit, but they were as much a part of us as our skins. And, unlike me, Meng Shouzhen was an adept shapechanger, modifying her garments from day to day to conform to the dictates of fashion.

I flung the severed fox tail down. "That's for my brother, whom you stole from our *louju* as my mother slept."

"Don't let her hurt me," she whined, casting pleading eyes at Bei Huangong. "I thought only to protect you, my darling stepson."

My husband stiffened, eyes unfocused and face slack.

"The same stepson you tried to lead to his death?" I recalled the thick scent of fox that night, the same fox-stink I smelled now. "You were that deer, *huli jing*. Did you also lure Bei Huangong's father over a drop-off? I think you did."

She snarled. "Clever rabbit. But not that clever." She fixed me with her golden, fiery eyes, confident she could snare me again—weak rabbit, easy prey. But I was *not* a weak rabbit. I was a fire rabbit. And my soul burned hotter and brighter than the feeble glints of her eyes.

I plunged the knife into her chest, and it sank to its hilt in her black heart.

"Even a rabbit will bite, if you corner her."

I yanked the knife free, and blood fountained over my hands. Meng Shouzhen sank to her knees. Fur bloomed on her face, her hands, and pointed ears sprouted through her hair. She crumpled, and the unmistakable body of a fox lay bleeding on the tile.

Spell broken, Bei Huangong startled awake. "My stepmother, a fox," he exclaimed, "and all this time we never suspected."

"Who knows what other animals might masquerade

among you," I said, my voice leaden. "Your wife might even be a rabbit."

He turned to me, stricken. "I'm so sorry, An-ying, so sorry for doubting you."

I met his eyes, and my heart ached. I longed to go to him, to rest my head on his chest and let all the ugliness that had transpired between us be erased in the security of his arms. Then I remembered my son's piteous body. Were he and my brother together in Huang-chuan, comforting each other while Mama sang to them?

"Your world is too complicated, too cruel for me," I said. "Even love is treacherous. You guard your hearts, wary of your affections. I thought once that my people bore the greatest burden of suffering, but I see now I was mistaken. My husband, you are sky and wind and rain to me, but I cannot bear the uncertainty of your love, always fearing it might be snatched away. Love is not a gift to be discarded, nor should it be held out as a goad or reward."

Bei Huangong buried his face in his hands.

I bent to retrieve my mirror and walked away. I padded barefoot over glazed tile, so much colder than grass and earth, passed beneath the double-arched ceiling, so much smaller than the sky, and strode into the garden. I mourned for the enslaved flowers, bullied and coaxed to conform to another's criterion of beauty. Slipping free of the stone walls, I wondered how I'd ever seen them as anything but an obstacle to the wind.

The moon was bright and full, Bótù's shadow clear. I raised my arms in wordless prayer, and the silvery light cleansed me, washing the blood and anguish and grief away. No longer a human maiden in a silk *ruqun* but a Daughter of Bótù once more—sleek fur, soft ears, and busy nose—I stood on my hind legs and gave thanks to the moon.

Buddha teaches that suffering ends when desire and craving are no more. All I had to do was renounce my heart's desire.

At the thud of footsteps at my back I swiveled, poised to fly.

"An-ying," Bei Huangong called, "An-ying!"

He sprinted to me. But I'd made my choice. I dropped to all fours and bounded away.

I once saw a rabbit on a hillside standing on its hind legs, gazing reverently at the full moon. Was it appreciating the view, moonstruck, or was it praying? Over time, I've come to regard the rabbit as something of a personal totem animal. I admire its grace and winsome features, its fanciful personality, and its mystical heritage. "Daughter of Bótù" was inspired, in part, by an ancient motif composed of three rabbits running in a circle, forming a triangle in the center, which has been found ornamenting architecture and artifacts across Europe and Asia. Its earliest appearance, on the ceilings of Buddhist cave temples, dates from the Sui Dynasty (581-618 CE), and it has appeared on Islamic, Christian, and Judaic icons as well. No one knows for sure where or when this symbol originated or what its original meaning was. Also, I think people underestimate rabbits. In the immortal words of Oz from Buffy the Vampire Slayer*: "they might not look it, but bunnies can really take care of themselves."*

The Tiger Fortune Princess

In addition to being as beautiful as a lily, the Empress of China, Meiying, was considered wise beyond her years. She honored her ancestors piously—burning fragrant incense and offering elaborate feasts up to them at every holiday—and thereby brought harmony and goodwill upon the Imperial Palace and all of China. When the auguries informed her she was pregnant with an imperial daughter, she was careful to read only soothing works of poetry, look at pleasing colors, and guard herself against outbursts of bad temper so her child would be sweet natured and wise.

As was the tradition, she had a soothsayer cast her unborn baby's horoscope. But as the final brushstrokes were laid on the paper, a servant girl was distracted by an errant flash of sunlight and spilled tea on the fortuneteller's composition.

This angered the soothsayer who demanded the girl be beaten for her clumsiness. But the young empress would not allow it.

The soothsayer narrowed her eyes and added an unlucky four more strokes to the tea-splattered paper, transforming the fortune into a curse. "Your daughter will die unborn unless she rides the dragon's tail," she hissed. "If she survives the dragon, she will be devoured before she meets her husband, and without a son-in-law, her father will die of unhappiness."

The empress furrowed her brow. With careful courtesy, for she would not harm her unborn daughter by changing the alignment of her own ch'i energy with an act of vengeance, she gave the soothsayer an envelope of money and escorted her to the palace gates.

As she watched the old woman stump away, the empress folded the fortune into a tiny square. She shared the fortune with no one, not even her husband, for that would give the words greater power and attract the attention of evil spirits. Returning to her bedchamber, she hid it in a jade locket carved into the shape of a leaping tiger.

Despite the inauspicious words of the soothsayer, it was still a favorable year to have a baby—the Year of the Dragon. No matter what else, the child would have dragon virtues: health, bravery, and splendor.

Time passed, and the date the midwives had declared as the most promising for the princess's birth came and went. The empress did not fret. She brewed special herb teas and tutored her mind to dwell upon serene thoughts of lucky, red fish swimming in sparkling waters and the perfect tranquility of white clouds floating in the azure sky.

"Your daughter is too much in love with the womb," the doctors said.

"Nonsense," the empress replied. And when they had gone, shaking their heads with disapproval, she murmured to her rounded belly: "I know waiting is difficult, my dear one, but do not listen to them." And she continued composing another devotion of patience to read to her unborn daughter.

Days melted away like sugar in the rain until it was the day before the New Year.

That morning, the empress had all the servants bring her scraps from their clothes and sewed these with her own hands into a patchwork coat. The servants looked at her as though her mind had taken flight, but the empress knew the coat would confuse any malicious demons. She draped the rag coat over her gravid body.

"Today is the last day of the year, the very tail of the dragon," she announced.

No sooner had the words left her lips than a great pain like a burning needle ran through her body. She cried out, and as morning strolled the path to afternoon, her daughter, Wen-Xiu, was born.

The servants ran to attend the child, but the empress waved them away. She checked the baby's heartbeat, and smiled when Wen-Xiu took her first breath and expelled it in a lusty howl. She was healthy as a dragon.

"Welcome, my daughter," she said. "And thank you for your patience."

To hold her daughter's soul to the world, Empress Meiying tied a tiny silver lock around the baby's neck with a bright red string. Then she bundled her up in the coat of rags and left the palace.

Meiying's husband, the emperor, watched them go with his heart drowning in a lake of sorrow. "But why must you leave?" he asked.

"I cannot tell you, but I have my reasons."

The emperor trusted his wife and so had no choice but to let her go.

The empress took Wen-Xiu to live in a tiny cottage, deep in the countryside, for she knew that bad luck demons would never think to seek out a princess in such humble surroundings. As further precaution, she stitched lucky, red cloth in Wen-Xiu's clothing to protect her from illness, tied tiny bells on her ankles and wrists to frighten evil spirits away, and looped a wide ribbon around her ankles to keep her steps steady so she would not fall and hurt herself. And every day she begged the ghosts of her ancestors to protect her daughter.

Wen-Xiu grew up to be graceful and clever, as splendid as her birth year promised. Even garbed in peasant rags, her beauty shone like a second sun. Her skin was as fair as the shining clouds her mother had contemplated in the palace, her lips red as crimson koi, and her black hair fell to her ankles in a glossy waterfall.

On Wen-Xiu's eighteenth birthday, a mounted servant from the Imperial Palace came to the door of their humble cottage with a racing horse saddled and in tow.

"My lady," he panted, "the emperor is gravely ill. They fear he will die."

Meiying grabbed her mantle and swung onto the prepared horse. "I must go to him."

"But Mother, why?" Wen-Xiu asked.

The empress took off the jade tiger locket she had worn for eighteen years and gave it to her daughter. "I have taught you and protected you as well as I can. Come to the Imperial Palace with your husband when you find him, my dear one. Your father's life and the Empire of China depend upon it."

And in the drumming of galloping hooves, she was gone.

Wen-Xiu opened the locket and read the tea-smeared words of the soothsayer and so discovered her regal identity and her fated doom. She began to cry.

The ghost of Wen-Xiu's great-great-grandmother, who was well pleased with all the offerings Meiying had burnt to her over the years, was close enough to hear her weeping. "Why are you crying, Granddaughter?" she asked.

"I do not want to die," Wen-Xiu said.

"Some events must happen as they must, and others, well, there may be allowances. Dry your eyes. You are the future of the empire, and you have a husband to summon."

Wen-Xiu dabbed the tears away with a corner of her sleeve, for she was as brave as she was beautiful. "How will I find him?"

"Do as I tell you. Put the fortune back into the tiger. Jade is a powerful stone, and the tiger is fierce and he will continue to protect your best interests. Next, take an apple and enclose him within it and cast both into the river. The tiger will return to you with a husband."

Wen-Xiu did as her ancestor instructed. She took an apple, gleaming red as a priceless ruby and as large around as a crane egg, and cut a sliver from the shining fruit. She ate the slice and affixed the locket in the white gash.

"May my soul take flight with this apple and bring my intended husband to my side." She threw the apple into the river, and as it flew from her hand, it was as though the world spun and she lifted into the air. For so long the fortune had been a cloak over her spirit, needing but her assent to become one with her soul. When it splashed into the water, it seemed that the sky covered Wen-Xiu's face and flung her down into an endless horizon of deepest blue.

She sank down as though she were dead.

Prince Quon-Yin and his huntsmen were riding along the shore when the prince felt fingers tweaking his hair. Unseen by the prince, these fingers belonged to the ghost of Wen-Xiu's great-great-grandmother. The prince turned his head in annoyance and saw what he thought was a ruby, floating on the sky-blue water. He watched it, and it grew to the size of a robin's egg, then a magpie's, and then finally a crane's. And then he saw it was not a ruby at all, but an apple.

He fished it out, and as soon as his fingers touched the firm, red skin, he was overwhelmed by a great hunger. Without pausing, he took a bite of the fruit. But curiously, he found he was even hungrier after swallowing it. He took another bite, and this time his teeth caught on something. It was Wen-Xiu's jade tiger locket.

Prince Quon-Yin opened the locket and read the fortune. His heart stumbled as he read the description of the beautiful princess, and his face darkened with grief when he read of her terrible fate. The need to rest his eyes upon the princess's loveliness blossomed in his chest like a flame-red orchid, putting even his hunger to shame. Without telling his companions of his intention, he turned his horse to follow the river.

The prince rode without pause until the sun god, Ri, resplendent in the white robes he wore to salute the dawn, had exchanged it for the somber saffron robes he wore in preparation to greet his wife, Yue, the moon. In the cinnabar light, Prince Quon-Yin saw a vision, bright as a shining cloud that had settled to earth. As he came closer, he saw that it wasn't a cloud but a maiden with pearl-white skin. Her hair wreathed her in a gleaming blanket of night as she lay by the riverbank, and her lips were red as cherries.

It had to be she, the tiger fortune princess.

He knelt by her side. "Princess?" To his great sorrow, she was not breathing. With trembling fingers, he opened the jade locket and extracted the fortune. Reading the terrible words again, he crumpled the smeared parchment in his hand and tore it to shreds. But his despair was not assuaged, so he popped the whole thing in his mouth and swallowed it.

As soon as the paper passed into his belly, Prince Quon-Yin's strange hunger was sated, and Wen-Xiu opened her eyes. The prince found himself staring into eyes as dark and mysterious as the most precious plum wine.

"Did my tiger bring you?" she asked.

"Indeed, he did," the prince replied. And he gave Wen-Xiu back her locket.

"And did you fight off the monster that was going to devour me?"

The prince grinned. "No, beautiful one. I ate the fortune. It would appear that *I* am the devourer."

Wen-Xiu considered this. "You have eaten my soul then, for surely it was trapped within that cursed parchment."

"And so I must return a soul to you the only way I may, by giving you mine. Marry me, and our spirits will be one."

Wen-Xiu blinked and then smiled. A laugh, bright as a

golden bell, pealed from her mouth. The lower tones of the prince's laughter swirled into the sky to join and mingle with hers.

The next day, they rode with all haste to the Imperial Palace where Empress Meiying watched over her ailing husband. As soon as they burst into his bedchamber, the emperor's sickness lifted from his soul, and he sat up, healthy and strong.

"Who is this whose presence heals me better than any doctor's balm or tincture?" he demanded.

Princess Wen-Xiu bowed. "I am your daughter, Wen-Xiu, and here is my husband-to-be, Prince Quon-Yin."

The emperor embraced his lost daughter and welcomed his new son. There was much rejoicing, and everyone in China was happy—except for one old soothsayer, who complained always of mysterious fingers that pinched her and pulled her hair so that she was forever mottled with bruises and quite bald. And never did a holiday go by that the imperial ancestors were not feted and praised for their compassion and wisdom.

I was born a month premature at the tail end of the Year of the Boar—demonstrating an early predilection for haste and impatience that only the publishing industry, with its protracted response times and interminable delays, has managed to pummel out of me. My mother told me that my early arrival was generally thought to be a good thing, as it appears there was some concern that I might be born in the Year of the Rat. Personally, of the two zodiac animals, I find rats more appealing than pigs, but I don't think that was topping my list of considerations when I demanded a venue change that night. Still, I'm glad my entrance into the world didn't distress any of my murophobic family members. Thus inspired by Chinese

cultural traditions and superstitions surrounding pregnancy, astrology, and ancestor veneration, "The Tiger Fortune Princess" is my Far Eastern spin on the classic "Snow White" and "Sleeping Beauty" fairy tales.

A Thread of Silk

Prologue

Sitting in the back on the Ōtemachi subway, away from the glitter of young people bedecked in late-night finery, the young woman gazed out the window as though fascinated by her reflection in the glass. She was indeed remarkably beautiful, but if anyone had looked beyond the flawless cream of her skin or the deep claret of her lips, they would have seen that her eyes were focused not on her image, but beyond it, as though they looked upon a time a thousand years away.

Mae peered through the thick shutter at the embattled men and wished she knew how her brother fared, whether Sadamori was safe. He was with Father, protected by many ranks of loyal Taira guards, defending the *seimon*, the main palace gate. But her brother was always one to take foolish risks, and this band of *bushi* was frighteningly well organized.

"Please, kindly kami spirits and benevolent ancestral ghosts," she whispered, "guard Sadamori."

A scuffle across the courtyard seized her attention. A Taira sentry fell, his blood a spray of black in the torchlit night.

In the breach his death created, one of the enemy *bushi* broke through the back gate.

Mae steadied her breathing as she nocked an arrow. She stepped into position and pulled the bowstring taut, sighting down the shaft's length. In her mind, a silk thread shimmered smooth and straight. The whimpers of the servants at her back faded to an insignificant buzz.

She released the arrow in a liquid motion, exactly as Sadamori had taught her. It pierced the man's throat at his armor's divide, and he half spun, dropping his *tachi*. The blood-streaked blade spun away on the cobblestones. He dropped beside it, kicking and writhing.

Behind her, Uma shrieked. "You killed him!"

"Quiet," Mae snapped. "Would you prefer it was your blood the God of War took instead of his?"

Uma sniveled, wringing her gnarled hands.

Outside, the arrow-downed *bushi* lay still. Mae shivered. Killing a man was nothing at all like hitting straw targets in the practice yard. She regretted scolding her old nurse. The poor thing was terrified; they all were.

"Mae-hime!" Seiichi, her father's head gardener, pointed at the wall. Another wave of intruders, weary of being curbed at the barricade's opening, were clambering over it.

Mae drew another arrow and swept all else from her thoughts until only the silk thread remained, bright and strong.

Her bolts picked two men from the wall. They fell, and she was glad for the earthen barrier that concealed their deaths. Then the invaders were over, and she dared not shoot for fear of hitting Taira men. They swarmed the defenders, a deadly infestation of steel stingers and armored carapaces. The line of battle grew closer, step by step, as the Taira gave ground, overwhelmed.

Mae shook so hard she fumbled the next arrow before she could nock it. It clattered to the floor, and she groped for another, rushing for fear of losing her shot. She knew as soon as the bolt leaped from the curve of her bow that it was bad, and sure enough, the point deflected harmlessly off overlapping tiles of armor.

Before she could bend, Seiichi was there, handing the dropped arrow to her. The gardener clutched his hoe, a resolute glint in his rheumy eyes. Mae smiled, both amused and touched.

"You think to hew down those *bushi* as though they were weeds, Seiichi-kun?" she murmured.

"Even the wishes of a small ant reach heaven," he retorted.

Mae set arrow to bowstring. "And surely, you are the loudest ant of all."

She chose a target, her hands steady once more. She did not flinch when the point found its mark, lodged in a *bushi's* eye socket, and she no longer resented that Sadamori had sent her to defend the servants instead of joining the archers at the *seimon*. It was not a dishonor, but her duty as Taira no Mae to protect her people.

Mae held the thread of silk in her mind, let it compose her movements and steady her aim as she sent one shaft after another into the fray outside. The thread eclipsed all else until there was no Mae, no shouting men, no fear. She reached for another arrow and was startled to discover only two left in her quiver.

No matter. There was her *naginata* when they were gone. The swordspear at her feet, with its shaft as tall as she and tipped with its fine steel blade, was as lethal as any *tachi*.

Mae squinted into the darkness, searching for her next quarry. She gasped, and the bowstring went slack in her fingers. Seiichi was out there, scrambling and hunched in the courtyard.

What was the old fool doing?

Heart filling her throat, she watched him retrieve an arrow, the first she had misfired, and then go after others, her misses and also ones lodged in still-warm flesh. He gathered them together like flower stems.

"Seiichi, you idiot," she moaned. "Get out of there!"

The gardener bobbed his head as though he could hear her over the tumult of combat, but he continued scuttling on ancient legs about his self-appointed task.

From the front of the palace, a twofold cry went up—a roar of victory mingled with anguish. A crash she could feel through her straw sandals proclaimed the news. The *seimon* had fallen.

The warriors in the courtyard, invaders and defenders alike, knew as well as she what those sounds portended. The insurgent *bushi* rallied as her father's men faltered—some even turning to flee, only to be struck down from behind.

In the chaos, one of the Taira guards, waving his *tachi* in wild arcs, blundered into Seiichi. Mae watched helplessly, an arrow ready to fly to the old man's aid. But she was unwilling to kill one of the palace defenders. The gardener, his arms filled with spent arrows, was swept off his feet. The *bushi* did not even pause but lashed out with his sword.

A cluster of red feathers—noblewoman's fletching—sprang from his neck. Mae did not remember loosing the arrow, nor did she spare a thought for the Taira man she had killed. She had eyes only for the crumpled gardener.

The shadows themselves paused as Seiichi stirred, as astonished as Mae that the old man still lived. He dragged himself to his knees and, unbelievably, began collecting the arrows he had dropped.

Tears rained from her eyes as Mae pulled her final arrow.

"Help him in," she cried. "Help him!"

Behind her, two grooms, and even Uma, scrambled out. While she covered them, they hauled Seiichi through the window.

Blood poured from a cut in his side, turning the undyed hemp of his kimono black. Mae slammed the shutter and barred it, muffling the sounds of violence from without.

Uma appropriated the arrows Seiichi stubbornly clung to while the others laid him on the floor.

Mae knelt. "You stupid old man," she murmured. "That was a very brave thing you did."

"Even an inchworm has five tenths of a soul." Seiichi coughed, and blood sprayed from his lips.

"Your soul is as big as a mountain."

Seiichi smiled. "I hope not. Then I might be the emperor's son in my next life instead of a humble gardener. I would miss my flowers."

"You will have many seasons to admire your flowers, Seiichi-kun, not in your next life, but in this one."

He coughed again, the sound like a choked fountain. "These eyes have seen their last bloom, but I am not afraid of Lord Death. Rather, I fear for you."

He pressed a crumpled scrap of cloth into her hand. It was a crest from the night-dark uniforms of the invading *bushi*. But instead of the broad leaves of the paulownia, emblem of the Minamota clan and sworn enemy to their house, it was the graceful butterfly of the Taira—the same insignia woven into Mae's kimono and stamped on her bow.

Mae inhaled. "How—?"

But Seiichi was gone, lured away by the blossoms in Lord Death's garden.

"Oh, Seiichi." Mae rocked the old man in her arms. Uma added her lamentation, keening like a mad seabird as she hugged the gore-drenched arrows.

Their grief was interrupted by the rattle of the interior bamboo screen thrust aside. Mae's head whipped up, and she pulled the glittering length of her *kaiken* from her sash.

Sadamori stood in the entrance, his armor giving his lean

form the shoulders and girth of a giant, and his *kabuto* helm the silhouette of a demon.

Mae cried out in relief. Letting her *kaiken* fall, she flung herself into his arms.

"Mae-chan, thank all the gods in heaven you're unhurt." Sadamori enveloped her in a metal embrace. "The palace is breached and our troops in rout. We must ride from here."

"Where has Father decided we are to fall back to?"

Sadamori shook his head, grim-faced. She knew by the way he pressed his lips together, as though to keep back the terrible news, that the most awful of outcomes had transpired.

"How?" she asked. "How did Father die?"

"Later, Mae-chan. We must hurry."

Mae relieved Uma of her burden of arrows and restored her *kaiken* to its scabbard while one of the grooms brought her the *naginata*. Hand-in-hand, brother and sister fled through the back corridors of the palace they had grown up in. A huddle of servants, frightened and silent, followed in their wake.

Outside, a regiment of Taira guards clustered, bows out and *tachi* drawn. They were few, and the ones that were not wounded were elderly *bushi* on the cusp of retirement.

"This is it?" Mae gulped, "all that is left of our house?"

"Shigemori-kun took two garrisons with him. He rides for Kyoto to appeal to the emperor." Sadamori boosted Mae into the saddle of a roan palfrey, her favorite.

"What does our brother hope to accomplish?" she asked.

"Nothing less than *rinji*, the emperor's personal edict of condemnation on this brutal and unlawful attack."

Sadamori oversaw the servants—even Uma, too scared to complain—being hauled up behind other riders before he swung atop his warhorse. At his signal, they galloped for the forest.

The estate was a nightmare of burned gardens and death. Mae shuddered and averted her eyes from the arrow-riddled corpses of Taira *bushi*, some with their eyes open and their faces twisted into rictuses of terror. There would be many angry ghosts in Hitachi Province after this night.

When they were free of the palace grounds and into the forest wilds, Sadamori slowed them from a headlong gallop to a gentle canter. Mae understood the need to save the horses, especially the ones bearing double burdens, but she wished for greater speed to put the war-ravaged visions far away.

She nudged her mare into step beside her brother. "Sadamori-kun, they were wearing Taira crests."

Her brother's face was an impassive mask. "It was Taira no Masakado."

"Masakado?" Mae had never met her cousin, although she recalled a fragment of some scandal—something to do with the emperor's birthday celebration in Kyoto. But she had never been one to follow the fickle peculiarities of courtly gossip.

"He has made a bargain with a demon." Sadamori's tone was as wooden as his face. "He brought a devil wind that always blew at his back, fouling our archers. I saw him fling aside strong, skilled *bushi* as though they were puppies, and he brought the *seimon* down with his bare hands. When Father saw this, he knew we were lost. He commanded Shigemori and me to retreat while he took a wedge of his best *bushi* to make a final stand, to keep their cavalry from overrunning the palace. His was an honorable death."

Mae reached for her brother's hand, and he clasped her fingers.

"I must avenge Father." Sadamori's voice quivered. "Little sister, I fear I will fail and bring dishonor upon our family."

"Sadamori-kun—"

"Arrows bounced off his flesh. He shrugged aside a cut from my own *tachi* that would have killed any other man. And, Mae, he wore no armor!"

"No armor?"

"Only a black *hitatare*. It was as though he were

mocking us, wearing silk undergarments to battle."

Mae felt the tremor in her brother's hand. "You must not fixate upon such things. The wise bee does not sip from a flower that has fallen."

The barest hint of a smile lifted her brother's lips. "That's something old Seiichi might have said."

"He was always ready with a proverb, wasn't he? I think he came up with them by the pageful as he puttered around with his watering can." Her eyes burned. "Poor old Seiichi."

"I will avenge him too. All our people who died tonight must be avenged so their ghosts may find peace."

Mae jerked on her brother's hand, making him face her. "*We* will avenge them, Sadamori-kun. Together."

He nodded. "Together."

Their destination was an old Shinto shrine in the forest, longtime haven to wartime refugees. By unspoken law, the sanctity of its grounds was inviolate.

A white-robed priest met them beneath the vermilion arch of the torii, the sacred gateway that marked the border between the physical world and the realm of spirits. He carried a lantern and seemed to glow by its light.

Sadamori dismounted and removed his *kabuto*. Mae frowned as she saw the discolored lump that swelled his forehead.

"Honored *kannushi*," Sadamori said, "I regret that we must pollute these hallowed premises with sorrow and strife."

The priest stroked her mare's velvet nose as Mae slid off her back. "The world is one great family, Taira no Sadamori-dono. While we *kannushi* aspire to avoid looking upon that which is not pure, it would constitute a shameful taint upon our hearts if we did not welcome our family home." He winked. "Just be so kind as to wipe your feet."

Before following their guide up the tree-lined path, brother and sister clapped twice and bowed three times in salutation to the attendant kami. Four ravens took wing as Mae stepped through the torii, roused from their perch on the crossbeam. She watched their flight, discomfited. It was well known that spirits were fond of expressing themselves through signs and portents, and while birds, especially ones perching on a torii, were auspicious omens, four was an exceptionally ill-favored number, associated with death.

Two more priests, a pair of bright banners in their chalk-white robes, descended the front steps of the shrine. They took charge of the horses with gentle insistence, ushering the wounded *bushi* and servants to a grove of trees. Mae and Sadamori were left to ascend the shrine's steps alone.

Built to harmonize with nature, the shrine's vaulted roof spread protective wings inviting kami to visit and shelter within. Inside, it was lit by several lanterns resting on burnished pillars. The altar was a simple affair of tiered shelves flanked by a pair of evergreen saplings and a bronze bell to summon the attention of spirits. The lower shelves held a pitcher of water, a jar of sake, and pots of both salt and rice—bulk containers from which the priests procured their daily offerings. At the apex stood the kami house—an unadorned cabinet with two doors.

Mae kneeled and bowed her head. Sadamori did not join her.

"Isn't it wrong to pray to the kami with a heart full of grief and a mind that longs for vengeance?" he asked.

"Perhaps. But I am also praying for our brother's safety."

With a great rattle and clatter of armor, Sadamori sank beside her.

In the silence of prayer, Mae snuck a glance at him. His normally cheery face had acquired lines of sorrow and worry. And he was so pale, the bruise ugly and stark at his brow.

"How did you get that bump?"

Sadamori reached a hand to his head and winced. "When

I struck Masakado with my *tachi*, he swatted me aside. I lay dazed—I'm not sure how long—until Shigemori-kun pulled me up."

"It looks tender."

"Masakado knocked me flying. If he'd used his fist, my skull would have caved in. As it is, I feel like there's an iron club at war with the inside of my head."

"Your skull's too thick to break." Mae stood. "Still, let me see."

She brought a lantern over, and Sadamori flinched at the tiny flame.

"Does this hurt your eyes? Are you dizzy?"

He scowled. "What do you expect with you waving that light in my face?"

Mae eyed the muted lamp, steady as a *kaiken* in her hand, and set it aside. "Does your stomach feel sick?"

"It always does after a battle."

She began unlacing the ties that held Sadamori's armor on.

"What are you doing?" he protested. "I can do this outside."

"It's a miracle you didn't fall off your horse after that knock to your brain. If you faint in your full armor, I won't even be able to drag you down the shrine steps."

"Don't be ridiculous. I'm not going to faint." Sadamori stood, but before he could take a step, he reeled, holding a hand out for balance.

Mae rushed to his side, taking his arm over her shoulders. "You dumb ox. What did I tell you?"

"He's a demon, Mae-chan," Sadamori muttered. "I'll throw parched beans at him next time." He slumped against her.

"That's not funny. Stand up." She jostled his arm. "Come on, Sadamori-kun."

He went limp, and she sprawled beneath his full weight.

"Sadamori, wake up. Sadamori!" Her voice turned shrill.

"Somebody, help!"

She heard the clatter of straw sandals on wooden floorboards. Several priests came running, their white robes flapping like great crane wings. With a few grunts and much awkwardness, they half-rolled, half-lifted Sadamori off.

One of them assisted her to her feet—the head priest who had greeted them at the torii. "What happened?" he asked.

"A blow to the head. I didn't know he was hurt. He showed no weakness at all during the ride." Mae enlisted their aid in removing Sadamori's armor, and they hauled him onto a straw mat. "My brother has always been like that, putting aside sickness and injury until either he conquers it, or it overcomes him." Her voice cracked, and she sucked in an unsteady breath. "*Kannushi*, why won't he wake up?"

"His soul is heavy, daughter. It bears a great burden of grief and pain. We must make him as comfortable as we can and wait for him to awaken when he is ready to."

The priests bustled out, leaving Mae to sit vigil. At first, Sadamori tossed and muttered to himself as though gripped by evil dreams. She hoped that whatever nightmares tormented him might also propel him out of the spirit realm, but as the lanterns burned low, his agitation stilled, and his breathing grew shallow.

The pallor of Sadamori's face terrified her; Mae couldn't bear to look at it. She stared instead with fixed obsession at the rise and fall of his chest. When he exhaled, her blood froze, fearful that that breath would be his last, and each time he inhaled, her soul warmed, and she thanked all the gods for the miracle.

As the night deepened, this circuit of despair, hope, and relief took its inexorable toll. Mae rose and stormed to the altar. She wrenched open the pot of rice and slung its contents at the kami house. Hurling the salt bin against the cabinet doors, she sent a shower of salt to mingle with the rice. She seized the pitcher of water, but blinded by either a mist of salt or the brine of her tears, her aim was off. It shattered above the shelf, spraying its contents over cabinet, rice, and salt. When she came to the jar of sake, she gulped several mouthfuls before pouring the rest onto the shrine's floor.

"There! You cannot say the offering is not enough," she shouted. "You have no excuse not to hear me, Bishamon. God of War, answer me!"

Her words echoed in the silence.

She picked up the bronze bell and struck it four times. "Bishamon! I'm calling you! Are you afraid of a woman's anger? Bisha—"

A wind howled through the shrine, extinguishing all the lanterns and hurling her to her knees. In the darkness, Mae pawed at her eyes, blinded by a faceful of sodden rice and salt.

When she could see once again, the shrine was no longer dark. A miniature cyclone whirled atop the altar, shedding a white-blue luminescence.

"I have come." The voice emanated from every corner—the exultant howl of the battlefield, the dangerous whisper of a new-drawn *tachi*, and the menacing thrum of a leaping arrow.

Mae fought her way to her feet, although the gale lashed her with a hail of rice and salt. "Take me instead," she called. "Let Sadamori live, and take me."

The wind lessened until Mae could stand without swaying like a drunken *bushi*.

"What makes you think I want you?" the voice boomed. "Or him for that matter?"

"Why else would you set Taira no Masakado upon us? We had no quarrel with him. Whatever our house has done to offend you, I offer myself to appease your wrath if you will let Sadamori and the rest of my family alone."

Laughter, like the clang of steel, ricocheted from wall to wall. "I have no grievance against you or your house. Taira no Masakado's sincerity impressed me; that is all. But now you have impressed me as well. I will give you a gift. Do you want what I gave him: invulnerability and the strength of seven men?"

"Yes!"

"Then you may have it. All you must do is take it from Masakado." The wind chuckled.

Mae stamped her foot. "You tricked me! I only wanted those so I could slay Masakado."

"Then you should have refused my offer and asked me to tell you how to defeat him." Still chuckling, the wind whirled away.

"Wait! You son of a worm! You—"

A clod of wind-strewn salt-rice flew into her throat and she doubled over, coughing. Between choked gasps, Mae used every *bushi* profanity she could remember overhearing.

"*Tch.* Such language." The voice was a woman's, melodious as a silk ribbon playing over the stings of a zither.

Mae spun around. The shrine, even though Bishamon was gone, was bright. But unlike his electric sheen, the air was tinged a festive red. The source of this new illumination came from the kami house. The cabinet was ajar, spilling radiance onto the strewn slop of offerings.

Mae swung open the doors. Red light splashed out, clinging like sticky bean paste to her hands and face.

"The God of War is not one for words, in any case," the voice continued. "Even angry ones. He prefers action. I, however, favor words. Although granted, it was your actions that attracted my attention—which is probably as well, considering."

"Benzaiten, Goddess of Love and Music," Mae breathed.

"I know who I am, child. Now, do *you* know what drew us here?"

"Anger at my desecration of the shrine?"

"Why should I be angry? I'm not the one who will be cleaning this up. Although I suspect the priests are going to be put out."

"Then, no."

"Sincerity, Taira no Mae. That which binds the divine to the mortal. The pureness of your soul's fury attracted the God of

War. But it is the intensity of your love for your brother and your selfless—albeit ridiculous—offer to trade your life for his that has earned *my* blessing."

"Can you give me the means to defeat Masakado?"

"I already have."

"I–I don't feel any stronger."

The goddess-light flickered. "It is not invulnerability or strength I have given you; those are not my virtues to bestow. But my gifts, in concert with Bishamon's, will surely conquer Masakado."

Mae scowled. "Bishamon didn't give me anything save his ridicule."

"Silly girl. He gave you the most important thing of all: knowledge. Think. 'You should have asked me how to defeat him,' he said."

Mae's eyes widened. "Which means Masakado can be defeated!"

"See? I knew you were clever. But are you certain this is the path you wish to tread? When War and Love come together, there is always suffering."

An image of Seiichi filled Mae's vision, his arms around a bouquet of bloody arrows. "I am sure."

"So be it. If you wish to defeat Taira no Masakado, you must set off for Sashima tonight."

"Tonight? Without Sadamori?"

"Indeed. Or else do not bother to set out at all."

"But why won't you heal him?"

"It is not up to me, or Bishamon for that matter, whether your brother lives or dies." The goddess's voice became a wisp of floating melody. "That is entirely up to him."

The red glow snuffed out. However, Love, being a more considerate god than War, relit a lantern as she departed, the one Mae had set by the altar. Its glimmer filled the kami house, flashing off the traditional mirror within. About to close the cabinet, Mae glanced in and was astounded to behold a stranger in the mirror gazing back.

She leaned close, dumbfounded.

Despite Sadamori's assurances to the contrary, Mae knew herself to be unremarkable. Her features were agreeable enough, but they were neither sophisticated nor striking. Yet her reflection was exquisite. Beneath lilting brows, eyes mysterious and charming as a cat's gaped back in disbelief, while velvety lips, red as plum wine, parted in astonishment. Mae pressed a hand to her cheek. In addition to being as white and lustrous as pearls, her skin was soft as orchid petals.

She peeked beneath her kimono. It was with a certain relief that she discovered the scar on her shin—from where Sadamori had accidentally clipped her, years ago as they practiced with *naginatas*—remained, as did the discolored patch on her forearm from when she had spilled a pot of scalding tea. Her spirit had not been deposited into a stranger's body, after all. Where her garments had stood between her skin and the goddess's light, she remained unaltered.

Sadamori stirred on his straw pallet, interrupting her astonished appraisal. Mae snatched the lantern and hurried to him.

She joggled him and called his name, but he still would not wake. It seemed the divine visitation had not roused him; at least he had come to no harm from all the flying rice.

"I must go now, Sadamori-kun," she whispered. "You better not die. If you do, I will kill Masakado all by myself, and you will be the laughingstock of everyone in heaven. 'Look at Taira no Sadamori,' they'll say, 'finished by a clonk to the head, and by a man his little sister dispatched, no less!'" Mae kissed his forehead. "So don't you dare die and leave me alone, you hear?"

She crept from the shrine. The moon had set, leaving the night sky wreathed in a star-spangled veil of wispy clouds. A suggestion of silver in the east hinted of dawn's unfurling banner.

"Taira no Mae-dono."

Mae gasped.

Behind her, silent and unseen, stood the head priest, his white kimono ghostly in the darkness. He held her mare's reins in one hand and Mae's bow, quiver, and *naginata* in the other.

"Please forgive me," he said. "It was not my intention to startle. I took the liberty of preparing your mount and weapons for your journey."

She swallowed back the thunder of her heart. "H–how did you know?"

The priest smiled. "Daughter, did you think we who serve the spirits and gods are deaf and blind not to notice Bishamon's ruckus?"

Mae's face burned. She accepted her weapons and secured them to her saddle. "*Kannushi*, I am shamed by how I have abused this holy place. I'm afraid I've made a terrible mess."

The priest chuckled. "It was not you alone responsible for the disorder within. Do not fret yourself. The kami are usually more subtle, as are we when we seek their attention, but perhaps when calamitous events are afoot, it requires a more candid approach. A day or two of sweeping and scrubbing will set things right."

Mae hoisted herself into the saddle. "Will you tell my brother I have gone to Sashima when he wakes?"

"Of course."

She bit her lip. "Do you think he will recognize me when he sees me?"

"Daughter, the mirror in the kami house is more than a symbol. Its purity and clarity teach us to look within and beyond. His heart will know to look past the bafflement of his eyes."

"I hope so. Thank you."

The priest bowed.

Mae turned her mare and sent her trotting down the path. As they passed beneath the torii, she squinted at the crossbar, but if there were any birds perched on it, they were hidden by the early morning gloom.

They picked their way through the forest while dawn spread a fan of pale pink, gold, and white across the sky. A stream twisted like a shining snake across their path. In the distance, the highway was still a dusty ripple—always closer as it peeped in and out between tree trunks.

Mae alighted while her mare drank and freed her hair from the band that secured it in an ankle-length train down her back. A shower of salt and rice pattered down, deposited from Bishamon's vehemence. Grains of rice were also trapped in the folds and layers of her kimono that no amount of shaking or brushing could dislodge.

As much as Mae desired to make all haste to Sashima, the gritty specks itched in a maddening fashion. And while she felt chagrined at postponing a blood vendetta to see to such luxuries as bathing, surely her cause would be better served if she came at Masakado with balanced focus, instead of distracted by her irritated skin.

Mae shed the outer layers of her kimono until she was clad only in the thin silk of her white *hitoe*. As her mare watched, brown eyes placid and amused, Mae brushed the folds of brocade until she was satisfied all the silty deposits had been displaced. Draping these robes over convenient boxwood bushes, she shrugged aside her *hitoe* and knelt by the stream. The chilly water raised prickles on her arms as she splashed away the residue Bishamon had flung over her.

A neigh brought Mae's head snapping up. Four rough-looking men abandoned their efforts at stealth and stepped from the foliage behind her.

Mae snatched her *hitoe*. Even as she clutched the silk to her breasts, she reproached herself for allowing modesty to usurp reason. Her *kaiken* hung on a branch two steps away. She ought to have scrambled for it, not the useless *hitoe*.

As though anticipating her intent, the first man drew his

tachi and flipped her *kaiken* spinning away.

"Good morning, *hime*." He grinned, displaying a gap of missing front teeth. "Have we disrupted your morning ablutions?"

"I haven't any money," Mae declared. "And my brother is just over the hill."

"He is? He can't be too protective of you as we came from that way, and we didn't see anyone."

The other men chuckled. One, bearing a scar across his nose, fingered the front of his *hakama* pants.

Mae shrank back.

"And who said we wanted money? We're collecting donations of silk. That's a very nice piece you've got there. Kindly toss it over."

She swallowed. "W–wouldn't you rather come here and take it?"

Gap-tooth's grin widened. He shoved his *tachi* back into its sheath and advanced. When he was close enough, Mae flung the voluminous length of her *hitoe* over his head and bolted for her mare.

Before she could spring into the saddle, a great weight smashed into her. She screamed as she went down beneath a snarling man. She thrashed, catching flesh beneath her raking nails before coarse hands pinioned her arms to the ground.

Gap-tooth's friend, Scar-nose, touched his bleeding face and scowled. He slapped her, rocking her head back.

The next moment, a tuft of red feathers protruded from his mouth. Scar-nose wore an expression of confused indignity as he toppled, his skull pierced by an arrow.

Mae rolled away and sprang to her feet. Sprinting the few steps to her mare, she yanked her *naginata* free and pivoted, wheeling it in a wide arc.

A man clad in billowing black parried aside the concentrated efforts of two of her assailants, his *tachi* a blur, while Gap-tooth charged his exposed back.

Mae hurtled forward, whirling the *naginata* in a precision sweep. Its length gave her the advantage of speed, and the curve of its blade was razor-edged. It sheered through Gap-tooth's hamstrings, sending him bellowing to the ground. She shifted her grip beneath the guard and brought the swordspear back in a graceful, lethal arc, splitting him from throat to groin.

Mae hefted the shaft of her weapon and swiveled to face her next foe. But there was no one left. The black-clad man stood unscathed with his *tachi* coated in blood. His two adversaries were cleaved open and splayed into macabre attitudes of death.

Mae blanched as she looked at the obscenity they had wrought, and a hair-fine trembling seized her. She had seen enough violence and death in the last day to harrow her dreams forever.

The man bowed, his eyes averted. "My thanks for your assistance, *hime*."

"I–I, um." With the mindless havoc of battle ebbing, Mae realized she stood naked before a stranger. She dropped her *naginata* and covered herself with her hands. Her trembling became a quaking that rattled her teeth.

Moving slowly, as though she might flee at an abrupt gesture, the man edged to a boxwood bush and retrieved her lavender over-kimono.

A droning started in her ears. Dimly, she was aware of the man draping the kimono around her.

"Are you hurt, *hime?*"

She shook her head.

"My men are ahead on the highway. If you are in need of an escort, I would be honored to offer you my services wherever you are bound."

The buzzing in her head grew until it obscured all else, blotting out both sound and light.

When Mae opened her eyes, she saw an expanse of pale blue overhead. At first, she thought it was the sky, but the perspective was marred by wrinkles and creases, and she realized it was the blue silk of a tarpaulin.

Mae sat with a start.

Across from her, cross-legged on a straw mat, the black-robed man was busy with cloth and oil, polishing the length of his *tachi*. The biting sweetness of clove oil filled the tent. Arrayed lengthwise, its blade already gleaming, her *naginata* lay positioned for her to seize and bring to bear, and at her right, her *kaiken* rested on a cushion within easy reach. It was a courtly gesture, giving her the martial advantage—her weapons primed and at hand, while his was in a state of unreadiness.

"You handled that *naginata* with much skill." He glanced up, then quickly returned his attention to his task. "Who taught you the ways of the warrior?"

"My brother." Mae tightened the neck of her kimono, conscious of how little she wore. The man was younger than she'd thought, his face comely and unlined. His thick hair, almost as long as her own, was secured from his face by a simple cord, leaving it to cascade down his back and disappear into the blackness of his kimono.

"Not . . . your husband?" His eyes darted up, and when they met hers, he flushed and looked away.

"I'm not married."

"I hope you will forgive my forthrightness, but, ah, are you entertaining suitors?"

Mae blinked, taken aback. "What?"

"B–because I have seen you unclad," he stammered. "And it would not be, that is to say, the d–dishonor, or rather, if we were courting—"

Mae wished she had one of the broad fans that the court ladies in Kyoto were always waving about so that she could hide her blush behind it. Instead, she let her hair fall in a curtain over her shoulder, shadowing her face.

"I don't even know your name," she said.

"I am Taira no Masakado."

Mae swayed, her thoughts awhirl. This was Masakado? She had expected him to be a brute of a man, an uncouth demon or sadistic fiend—like the hoodlums he had rescued her from— not an appealing youth with elegant manners.

"Are you unwell, *hime*? You've gone ashen."

"No, no, I'm fine." She loosened her grip on her kimono's neck, letting it slip apart to reveal the vulnerable expanse of her throat. "Your proposal is generous and honorable, but my circumstances are difficult." It was easy to let her voice catch and her lips tremble; she did not require pretense.

He set aside cloth and blade. "Has someone dishonored you? My *tachi* is yours to redress any insult."

She peeked at him through the screen of her hair as she gathered her thoughts, composing her tale. "Perhaps you will not be so quick to pledge yourself to me after you hear my circumstances. I am Kikyou no Mae," she lied. "My uncle is a powerful man, and also wicked and corrupt. He killed my father in an act of treachery, and in order to secure his claim on my father's estate, he demanded I marry him." She bowed her head. "I fled, for I would slit my own throat before I allowed him to defile me, but I have nowhere to go and no one to avenge my father's murder."

Masakado surged from his seat to kneel before her. "*Hime*, let me avenge your father's death."

There was such passion in him, such guileless fervor. "My uncle is a powerful man," she said, "with many legions of *bushi* at this command."

"I am not without martial resources. The God of War himself favors me."

Mae laughed, letting an edge of derision tinge it. "That is what my uncle boasted when I railed my grief at him."

Before she knew what he was about, Masakado drew her

kaiken and imprisoned her hand between his and its hilt.

"Can your uncle do this?"

With a sharp thrust, he plunged the honed knife at his chest, dragging her along with the force of his strike. Though it sheared through the thin silk of his *hitatare*, the *kaiken* left him unscathed, only skidding across his torso as though it was a plate of metal.

Awed, she reached her other hand through the tatters of silk. "How can this be? Are you some demon made of steel?" His skin was warm and pliant beneath her fingers.

Masakado covered her hand with his. She felt the throb of his heartbeat beneath her palm.

"Only a man." He bent his head, bringing his mouth to hers. His kiss was a blend of imperious demand, appetite, and tenderness—overwhelming even as it thrilled.

Breathless, she pulled away. "Blades do not rebound off men. How did you come to such an unnatural state?"

Masakado drew her back. "I told you; I am favored by the God of War." He buried his face in her hair.

She shivered. "Did you deliver me from rape so that you could force me yourself in the luxury of your tent?"

He released her. "I had not realized you found my company so repellent."

Mae bit her lip. Had she misplayed her strategy? Or merely wounded his pride?

She leaned close until her mouth hovered above his, separated by the space of a whisper. "Surely you know I do not find you repellent," she murmured. "Do not be angry with me, Masakado-dono, but you frighten me. I need some reassurance that you are not a rapacious demon."

Mae wavered between apprehension that he would not succumb to her enticement and trepidation that he would. This man was compelling, and his desire provoked a response in her so engulfing she wondered whether she acted from artifice or desire.

Masakado held himself rigid for a heartbeat and then relented, his mouth hungry as he kissed her. "Anything. Ask me anything. What can I offer to reassure you?"

Mae fought against the languid heat that fogged her mind. "Prove that you are still a man. Tell me how you are mortal."

He gazed at her, frowning.

She rushed on. "For if, as you claim, you are only a man, you must still have some softness, some imperfection. If you love me, a–as I love you, share this vulnerability with me and set me at ease."

His eyes were hard as they regarded her. "There is a spot behind my left ear where Bishamon rested his thumb that did not receive his anointing light." He yanked off the lavender brocade of her kimono and clamped her to the hard length of his body. "That is my vulnerability." He pulled her down. "I assure you, I am still only a man."

Mae lay across Masakado's chest, her kimono draped over them in a tangle of silk. She ached as though she had spent a day sparring on the practice field. Masakado had been a considerate lover, solicitous of her innocence, but also a demanding one.

She ran her fingers over his face, slack in sleep's grip, and touched the spot behind his ear where he had promised he was pervious. What if he had lied? Had she been a fool to take him at his word? How much honor could he have, the man who had led the massacre on her house?

Masakado stirred. He smiled and kissed her palm. "When we arrive at Sashima, I will have a priest marry us, Mae-chan. You will be my empress."

She arched an eyebrow. "Now you are the emperor?"

"I will be *Shinnō*, the New Emperor. It is why I and my

army march through Hitachi Province. I will overthrow the Old Emperor, taking his domain province by province."

Mae rose, wrapping her kimono around her nakedness. "You must hate him very much."

He caught the trailing edge of lavender silk. "The emperor's rule is decadent and wasteful. He encourages the clans to war and squabble while he fills his days with poetry and music. It is a weakness that will bring the empire to ruin."

"How does it strengthen it, creating more strife in the countryside?"

"In order to heal, sometimes the surgeon must cut. Last night, I overthrew the governor of Hitachi, a man of my own clan, so that all would know that I am not merely perpetuating the feud between Taira and Minamota."

"You brought down a whole house as a warning?" She turned away so he wouldn't see her face.

"That is the nature of war. Better they die than the empire. The governor was loyal to the emperor and would never have yielded. Rather than subject him to the humiliation of capture, I gave him an honorable death in battle. And I allowed his heirs to escape, though my captains urged me to finish them as well."

"I am sure they are grateful for your compassion," she snapped.

"It does not delight me to sow grief and lamentation."

"And yet you do."

"You are a woman and do not understand politics." Masakado stood and pulled on his *hakama*. "If you are able to ride, I will tell my *bushi* to break camp. I'm afraid I don't have a palanquin for you to take your ease in."

"I regret that my presence has delayed your subjugation of the empire, Taira-dono," she said coldly.

He scowled and stalked out.

Mae contemplated her *kaiken* where it had fallen, forgotten in their lovemaking. It would not take much strength to plunge it into the dip behind a man's ear; even a woman might do it.

Masakado swept back in. Guilt and surprise brought her spinning around, a cry on her lips.

He frowned. "Your mare is being saddled. We ride as soon as you have dressed."

Only then did she notice the armful of brocade and silk he carried. When she made no move to go to him, he deposited her clothes on the straw mat and turned to go.

Masakado paused at the tent's entrance and spoke over his shoulder. "Mae, you needn't fear me. No matter what, I could never hurt you."

The next days passed in a monotony of travel, the countryside flowing beneath the jingling hooves of a sea of cavalry.

Mae had ample time to study her enemy. Masakado was an enigma, two different people by sunlight and starshine. Around his men, during the day, he was always courteous to her, the epitome of polite consideration. His troops adored this Masakado, their eyes shining with devotion as he rode among them. He ate with his *bushi*, treating even the lowliest groom with respect, and in turn demanding and receiving unwavering obedience. But he was also aloof, curt and impatient if she intruded upon his thoughts. It was easy to hate him then, the arrogant tyrant and the callous butcher. In the clarity of the sun's splendor, her course was obvious; she must dispatch him with her *kaiken* as he slept.

But when the forthright sun stepped aside, making way for the moon, Masakado metamorphosed into her lover. With his army shut out by walls of silk, he made love to her with single-minded intensity, spurring them both to exhilarating peaks of ecstasy. Afterwards, as they lay sweaty and replete, he chatted with her as though to an equal, soliciting her opinion on wide-ranging topics. For one opposed to the emperor's preoccupation with the arts, Masakado had a nobleman's appreciation for philosophy and poetry. He was attentive and indulgent, making her laugh with his imitation of one of his captains, and infinitely tender, cradling her in his arms as he drifted into Lord Sleep's realm.

Every night as she lay in the circle of his arms, she remembered her resolve beneath the sun, and she told herself she would kill him the next night.

Days turned to weeks, and engrossed in her turmoil, she was taken aback to discover that they had arrived at their destination: Sashima.

The locus of Masakado's prefecture was a sprawling palace, almost as large as the emperor's in Kyoto. When Mae alighted, her heart was a lump of iron. It knew, as surely as the sky was vast, that the stolen hours of the night when Masakado had belonged only to her were over.

As soon as they stepped though the *seimon*, a *bushi* ran to Masakado with a folded missive. Mae saw the imperial seal; she knew what it heralded before Masakado announced it to his men.

Shigemori had been successful in eliciting the emperor's *rinji*. The emperor had assembled all the clans into a vast army that marched to Sashima, united in one cause: to annihilate Masakado. Furthermore, this host was led by her brothers, Shigemori and Sadamori—fully recovered from his injury.

Mae saw little of Masakado after that, as he was busy readying his estate for siege. He still came to her at night, but his lovemaking was urgent, almost desperate, and he often left afterward to return to some defense preparation.

On her own, Mae took to riding through the Sashima forest, meditating in the kami shrine ubiquitous to all estates or rambling through the overgrown trails.

One afternoon, when she arrived at the stable to fetch her mare, she found a piece of parchment tied to her bridle. It bore the Taira crest and the unmistakable pillars and crossbar of a torii.

Mae stared at the ink torii for a long moment, then bounded into the saddle, whipping her mare to a gallop. She made all speed to the Sashima shrine, her heart galloping faster than her mount's fleet hooves. Beneath the faded arch, she slid from her mare's back and sprinted up the path.

The shrine was a place of shadows and darkness. Abandoned long ago by any priests, it was crumbling apart. The shelves of its altar listed, and its offering plates were barren of even a lonesome grain of rice.

A figure stepped from the shadows. "Mae-chan? Is that you?"

"Sadamori!" Mae pelted to her brother and launched herself into his arms.

He hugged her, swinging her around in a dizzying circle. His laughter was a thunder of joy, and hers twined with his in a gale of elation.

At last, he set her down, cocking his head and squinting. "The priest said you would look different, that the goddess had touched you. But I didn't expect—that is, you look very fine," he finished lamely.

Mae giggled. "I'm still me."

"I know. I can see you the way you were if I sort of look sideways, but it's disconcerting to have such a dazzling sister." He pinched her cheek.

She swatted his hand away. "You'll get used to it. But Sadamori-kun, what are you doing here?"

His face turned serious. "The emperor's army is camped a day away. I begged him to postpone the assault so I could find you." He took her hand, leading her out. "Now that I have you safe, we will attack at dawn."

Mae pulled away. "I can't."

Sadamori turned, surprised. "It was very brave of you to go after Masakado alone. No one expects you to defeat him by yourself. Nevertheless, your information will be valuable. I assume you scouted the weakness of his troops like I taught you?"

"Not . . . his troops."

Her brother knew her too well. Sadamori gripped her arms. "Why do you hesitate?"

She could not meet his eyes.

"Mae, why are you crying?"

She brushed away the betraying tears.

Sadamori's face turned ugly. "Did Masakado abuse you? Force himself on you?" His fingers dug into her. "I will kill him, raze Sashima from this world, and obliterate his cursed name from the heavens."

"No, no. I–I was willing."

He released her so sharply she stumbled back. "What do you mean? Did he cast some evil spell over you?"

"He's not evil. Just a man."

Sadamori turned his back. "The day you were born was one of the greatest joys I hold in my heart." His words were harsh, ground out through clenched teeth. "I remember how you toddled after me, your eyes bright with adoration."

"Sadamori-kun—" Mae reached out.

"You have dishonored yourself, shamed me, and disgraced our ancestors. By rights, I should run you through with my *tachi*, or strangle you here and now."

Mae stepped back, her hand falling away.

Sadamori wheeled; his eyes were wet. "But I can't, to my eternal disgrace. I have always cherished you, and by the love I bear you, I cannot bring myself to harm you. But if you know something that will give us an advantage over that demon, you need to tell me."

Mae bit her lip, mute.

He glared helplessly. "Very well. When the emperor's *bushi* attack, I will be in the first ranks. I plan to kill Masakado or die honorably in the attempt. One of us will die, him or me. If you have any honor left, you will pray for me."

Sadamori stormed out.

Mae sank against the altar, hugged her knees to her chest, and sobbed.

When Mae blinked open her tear-crusted eyes, it was dark. She had fallen asleep, and the day had passed without her. Her limbs were stiff and cold, and she felt numb inside, as though a kami had stolen away her worry, terror, and confusion, leaving her empty. Through the holes in the thatched roof, the sickle moon crested the night sky.

How long had she slept?

Mae sat, brushing leaves and dust from her hair, and then wandered down the shrine steps. Her mare clopped to her, missing her dinner of grain and bed of straw, and eager to be away.

The palace's *seimon* was still down when they arrived, a flurry of *bushi* darting back and forth, engaged in last minute preparations. She gave her steed over to one of the grooms who, strangely, would neither speak nor look at her.

Puzzled, she made her way to the chambers she shared with Masakado. As usual, he was absent. But then, with the emperor's army on the brink of attack, she expected he was preoccupied. She untied her sash and began peeling off the layers of her kimono.

The bamboo screen rattled aside, flung open with such

force that it jumped its guiding rail and hung askew. Masakado stood in the doorway. Under one arm he had his *kabuto* helm; in the other he gripped her bow and quiver.

"So you decided to come back?" he snarled "Or did you just return for these so you could shoot me in the back?" He flung her weapons at her feet.

She glanced at them and shrugged, turning her attention back to folding her overcoat. "Not that an arrow in the back would be all that troubling to you."

Masakado glowered.

"You do not notice my comings and goings most evenings, Taira-dono. I apologize if I have inconvenienced you."

He took two strides to her and spun her around. "Did you tell your brother how to kill me?"

"What are you talking about?"

He shook her. "Did you think me stupid, Mae, when you came to me with the Taira crests on your kimono and emblazoned on your bow? Or that I wouldn't notice that you never mentioned your 'evil uncle' again?"

She plucked at his hands, annoyed at being jostled. "If you knew, why didn't you say anything?"

"I wanted to give you a chance to know me and perhaps to love me. But I was a fool, wasn't I? When my groom alerted me that he had seen Taira no Sadamori skulking about, and then you had ridden out so precipitously, I did not expect to see you again."

Unperturbed, Mae met the savagery in Masakado's eyes. "Are you going to kill me now? This might be your last chance. The emperor's army arrives at dawn."

He uncurled his fingers, allowing her to pull away. "I should. But I told you once I could never hurt you. That will never change."

"Funny, Sadamori wanted to kill me too, but he couldn't either. Lucky me, I suppose."

Masakado slumped to the floor, his head in his hands.

n echo of his scornful words in the shrine. *Do you want invulnerability and the strength of seven men? All you must do is take it from Masakado.*

Taira no Mae howled—a wail of bleakest despair and impotent rage.

Epilogue

The young woman got off the subway at exit C5, the journalism district, and turned into an incongruous courtyard nestled between the soaring glass and steel skyscrapers. A tall marker sprouted atop four stone steps surrounded by a modest hedge of saplings and bushes. Several stone frogs stood guard, and recent offerings of fresh flowers ornamented the site.

The woman scanned the vicinity. The hour was late, and most citizens—businessmen and revelers alike—were asleep. When she was sure there was no one to see, she set her shoulder to the headstone and pushed.

It was a most peculiar act. She was a slim woman and the stone was heavy and thick. But as she strained, the first step ground aside, creating a thin breach into darkness. The woman gave another furtive glance around and hopped in.

Beneath the Tokyo street, she took a small flashlight from her purse and used its wan beam to locate a granite box the size of a picnic hamper. She raised the heavy lid as though it weighed nothing and reached inside.

"Hi, Masakado," she said.

She lifted out a man's head, severed cleanly at the neck. Despite the violent truncation, it was couth, bearing no signs of decay or putrefaction, with the handsome features of a young man.

The eyes opened and the mouth moved. The woman leaned close, for without lungs or a diaphragm, the head's speech was silent. But she was proficient at reading lips and

"Did you ever love me?"

She shrugged. "I couldn't kill you. Does that count? I thought about it every day, how I would slip my *kaiken* under your ear. That seems to be what love is, not killing someone you should." She selected a wooden comb and ran it through her hair. "I thought Benzaiten the kindlier god over Bishamon, but I was wrong. She's a bitch."

"What do you want of me?"

"Everything. But nothing you can give me. I want that you hadn't assailed my home and killed my father. And that you had listened to your wise captains who advised you to finish us off. If you hadn't been so merciful, I wouldn't be damned, trapped between honor and love. But you can't change the past, can you?"

"Mae—"

"And even if I begged, you won't give up your stupid campaign and escape with me. You could, but you won't."

Masakado stood. "My *bushi* would be slaughtered without me."

"As I said, nothing you can give me."

He was silent, watching her tidy her hair. The dismal look in his eyes disconcerted her, and she gave him her back.

"What will you do now?" he said at last. "If you wish, I can arrange an escort to take you to your brother."

"Everyone keeps telling me to go to him."

His hands settled on her shoulders, and he gently brought her around. Masakado gazed at her as though he might hold her forever with his eyes.

"Leave or stay. It has always been your decision." His hands fell away, and he walked out the broken screen. On the floor, where he had dropped it, was his *kabuto*.

The stars blinked out, one by one, as the night sky lightened to the hesitant silver of pre-dawn. Outside, the din of the emperor's forces approaching crescendoed.

Mae strung her bow and slung her quiver over her shoulder. No one tried to stop her as she climbed the steps to the lookout above the *seimon* and joined the archers.

The emperor's army was a surging wave of violent resolve. It crested the *seimon*, broke on it, and fell back, only to regroup and smash against it again. Arrows churned like sea foam, bringing down *bushi* on both sides. Beside her, men sped shafts into the melee and were picked off in turn.

Mae neither nocked an arrow nor concerned herself with incoming bolts. She knew the gods were not so kindly as to allow her the ease of such a death. And indeed, though *bushi* all around her died, not a single arrow touched her.

Alone with the dead, she watched the battle spin out. The sun picked out Masakado, unburdened by armor, as he slashed with his *tachi*, wickedly nimble. He seemed a god with his hair a cape of darkness at his back.

On the other side, Sadamori was resplendent in full armor. Mae recognized the rhythm of his combat style; it was as familiar to her as her own steps. Her brother had taught her strength and strategy with *naginata* and bow, and by his encouragement, he had given her courage.

"Bishamon," she whispered, "would it be so much to ask you to keep them apart?"

As though to mock her, the *seimon* crashed down. Sadamori was one of the first through the gate. He called to Masakado, a cry so ferocious even she heard it from where she watched.

Masakado gestured and his *bushi* parted, letting Sadamori come.

"Typical," Mae sighed.

The collision of their *tachi* rang over the tumult. Sadamori attacked like one crazed, hammering at Masakado

with frenzied abandon. The ferocity of his assault seemed Masakado by surprise and smashed through his guard, or deflected by his skin. Masakado reeled from a ringing his head. It seemed that while he was impervious to *ta* he still felt the battery of their impact.

Sadamori was not stupid. He pounded his swor his foe, dazing him with blows that would have choppe man apart.

Mae snatched an arrow from her quiver. Nocki pulled the bowstring taut and fixed her eyes on the Sadamori's armor.

She summoned the silk thread, holding it in her

Masakado swung his *tachi* in an incredible arc, Sadamori's next blow. His return swing caught her *kabuto*, hurling Sadamori from his feet.

Sadamori landed in a clatter, his sword flying hand.

Masakado raised his *tachi* for the deathblow.

Mae loosed her arrow, and the bowstring snap the sound like a cracking whip. The arrow flew as she it, burying itself behind Masakado's left ear.

Masakado crumpled, his hair splayed behind h broken wings of a raven. Sadamori scrambled for Gripping it two-handed, he drove it down on Masaka cleaving head from body.

Mae set aside her useless bow. In a single, sw she drew her *kaiken* and slashed it across her throat. for the spurt of blood, the shock of pain, and blessed d

There was nothing. No blood, no pain, no deat

Uncomprehending, she stared at her *kaiken* gleamed, clean and bright. How had she missed her She tried again, this time using her other hand to cutting edge over the vein by her jugular.

Still nothing.

Bishamon's voice materialized out of the ba

expert at interpreting these particular lips.

"You look beautiful as ever, Mae," the head said. "Has it been a year already?"

"You know it has."

"How are little Misako and Ryoichi? Are my grandchildren well?"

Although there were significantly more generations than one separating Misako and Ryoichi from Masakado, Mae didn't correct him. As point of fact, she had forgotten herself how many "great"s should preface "grandchildren."

"Little Misako is in Cambridge, studying to be a doctor. Ryoichi is still writing his book on the Heian period. His publisher is annoyed with how long he's taking."

Masakado's head grinned. "He takes after you."

Mae stuck her tongue out. "He also refuses to compromise with his editor, the hardhead. He gets that from you."

"So he does. Whenever he gets it published you will bring it so I may see it?"

"Of course."

"Good. I quite enjoyed hearing the CD of Misako's violin recital you brought last year."

"How are you doing?" she asked. "Are you still content?"

"When I sleep in the dark, it is as though my spirit flies over the empire, protecting and watching over it. The gods have set me this task so that I may have these nights with you. It is just, and I am satisfied. And yourself, are you well?" The question was hesitant.

Mae smiled. "You always sound as though you expect me to flip out again. I'm fine." When she had discovered that she did not even have Masakado's weakness to deliver her to death, she had gone mad, shrieking and tearing her hair, her mind escaping the only way it could. But her body had summoned her back to tend to the new life it incubated,

Masakado's daughter.

She stroked the smooth skin of his face. "I miss you, though. I pine the whole year, longing for this night to arrive, and it's over so quickly."

"Mae-chan, don't mourn the time we do not have, but rather rejoice in the time we do. We will have a lifetime of years in these nights. It is simply the day that stretches between that is long."

Mae pressed her forehead against Masakado's. "The days are *very* long."

"And the night is short. Are you going to spend it lamenting what we cannot change?"

"You're a callous old man."

"And you're a crotchety old woman."

Mae chuckled, and Masakado's head laughed silently with her.

They chatted for a while, on serious matters and light; she told him a new joke she had found on the Internet; he told her a story from his childhood. Then they sat without speaking, only gazing at each other.

Far too soon, the alarm on Mae's cell phone buzzed, harbinger of the encroaching dawn.

She closed her eyes and kissed Misakado's mouth. Almost, for a moment, she could feel his arms holding her close and his body, warm and strong against her.

"Rest well, my love," she whispered.

"My dreams will be of you."

She set the head with infinite care into the stone box. When the features crumbled to dry ruin, a blackened skull with shreds of clinging skin, she replaced the lid and climbed out of Masakado's tomb.

As she shoved the stone step back into place, she was overcome by a swell of sadness; she missed him already. Mae knelt by the headstone, tidying the offerings her passage had disordered, and took comfort in remembering what he had said.

She would see him again tomorrow night, three hundred and sixty-four days away.

"A Thread of Silk" was one of my first forays into the rich arena of historical fantasy. Taira no Masakado, a lord of the Taira clan, lived in Japan during the Heian period in the middle of the 10th century. He revolted against the emperor, conquered several provinces, and appointed himself as the New Emperor before being killed and beheaded at the Battle of Kojima by his cousin, Taira no Sadamori. Today, the Japanese revere Masakado as a guardian spirit of Tokyo and have raised several shrines to him. The main one, in the Ōtemachi section of Tokyo, is also his tomb, the resting place of his severed head. For an insurrectionist who had his head lopped off, I figure that's doing pretty good.

The Snow Woman's Daughter

When I was a little girl, I thought my mother's name was "Yuki," which means "snow." That was part of her name, but I didn't learn the rest of it until the night my father died.

My mother left us on a slate-gray evening when I was five, with her namesake falling from the sky and piled high around the windows and doors. Awakened by raised voices, I watched through a tear in the curtain that shielded my sleeping mat as my mother wrapped her limbs in a shining, white kimono. As far back as I could remember, she had always worn the dark wool shifts that all mountain people wear, spun from the hair of the half-mad goats that give us milk and cheese. In her kimono she looked like a princess, or a queen. Her skin was paler than mine, and I am thought quite fair. Roku, the boy who lived on the northern crest, used to tease me when we were little, calling me "ghost girl" and "milk face."

That night, my mother was so white it was as if a candle shone within her breast. It made my eyes crinkle as I squinted through the thick cloth.

I saw her come toward me, and I scrambled to return to

my mat. She wasn't fooled, but then, she had never been deceived by my tricks.

"Sekka," she said, "I am going away."

I sat up, dropping my pretense. "Where are you going, Mama?"

"I am returning home. Your father broke a promise to me."

Through the swept-back curtain, I saw Father huddled miserably by the fire.

"When are you coming back?"

"Never."

The finality of her reply stunned me.

"But if you need me," she continued, "call my real name three times, and I will come for you."

"Your real name?"

"Your father will tell you what it is."

Her arms were cool as they embraced me. Soothing and restful when I was sick with a fever, now they chilled me through.

She pulled away from me, and I began to cry. I trailed after her, frightened and cold. Through my tears, I watched her open the door of our house, dressed only in the thin, white silk of her kimono. The breath of winter rushed in, sucking away the cozy warmth of our hearth fire. She stepped into the snowstorm raging outside.

I wanted to run after her, but Father caught me in his arms, and we both watched my mother walk away, melting into the whiteness of the falling snow.

I asked him that night what my mother's real name was, as I intended to call her back immediately. But he didn't tell me.

I asked him every year on the anniversary of that night until I was sixteen. He would not relent, and eventually the worries and uncertainties of a maiden approaching womanhood overshadowed family mysteries.

Most pressing of these was Roku. Somehow, between

rambling trips together to the market and snowball fights among the trees, he had become more than the brat who tugged on my braids and poured ice water on my head. My heart tripped and fluttered when our fingers brushed together, and heat filled my cheeks when he remarked upon the ribbon I had sewn to my skirt.

The intervening years had not been good to my father, though. He had withered from a strong, healthy figure to a feeble shadow, a wraith of a man. He merely blinked when Roku came one day, bearing a sprig of wild honeysuckle, and asked to wed me. It was as though the betrothal of his only daughter was of no more consequence than a discussion of the weather.

I had always assumed I would marry, but it had been a distant eventuality. Now I was as bewildered as if I had woken on a December morning to discover summer skies and the snow all melted away. How could I leave my father, our home, and become a wife and mother?

After Roku left, my father slumped in his chair before the fire. He pointed at Roku's engagement bracelet, heavy on my wrist, and said, "There drops my last excuse. The day I have always dreaded, when I must lose you, too, is nearly arrived. So tonight I will tell you your mother's real name."

Forgetting my trepidation about my impending marriage, I sat at my father's feet, waiting.

"When I was a boy," he began, "I was apprenticed to the woodcutter, Mosaku. One evening, we were out in the forest chopping logs, and a sudden blizzard overtook us. We ran into a tiny cave for shelter and prayed for the storm to end.

"Mosaku fell asleep. Eventually, I drifted off, too, and I dreamed.

"In my dream I saw a beautiful woman. Her kimono was made of ice crystals, and it glistened on her body like a sheet of diamonds. Her face was like the moon, cool and impassive, and her eyes flashed like sunlight on the snow.

"She bent over Mosaku and breathed out white smoke. It

covered my old master, sheathing him in a layer of spangled silver. Turning from him, her eyes fell upon me.

"I wanted to shout, cry out, but I was dazed by fear. I watched her walk to me, each footstep as graceful as a dancer's. She leaned close to my face, and I was sure I was going to die.

"'I had intended to kiss you as well,' she said in a voice as smooth and flawless as a pane of ice. 'But you are so handsome with your wide eyes and strong shoulders. I will spare you, but you must promise never to speak of me. If you even whisper of so much as the hem of my kimono, I will know it, and I will return to blow my kiss of everlasting sleep over you. Do you promise?'

"I nodded, and she was gone. I startled awake and saw poor Mosaku, quite dead. By then the snowstorm had stopped, and I fled home.

"Everyone asked me what had happened, and I told them we had been caught in the snow. I did not mention my dream of the white maiden with her breath of frost.

"The next year, I met your mother at the winter festival. She said her parents had died and she was looking for work as a servant girl. But her hands were far too pale and soft for the harsh work of a washerwoman. I invited her to be my wife, for I had fallen in love with her quiet voice and laughing eyes. She agreed, and the next week, we wed.

"Of course, she was the snow maiden in disguise. At first, I did not recognize her without her white kimono. But the chill of her arms and the pallor of her skin, who else could she be?

"I remembered my promise to her, and for six years, I said nothing. Then one night, as she was sewing a torn shirt for me, I saw her in the firelight, and her skin was whiter than lilies, and her eyes danced brighter than the flames. I was overwhelmed by love for her and could not believe how fortunate I was. How could someone as beautiful, as elegant as she, love a common woodcutter like me? In my stupid insecurity, I asked her:

"'Do you ever regret sparing me, that night in the cave?'

"I had not expected her to react so harshly.

"She flung down her sewing. 'You promised never to speak of so much as the hem of my kimono!' she shouted. 'You broke your promise! I should kill you for that, but for the sake of Sekka, I will spare you.'

"I was frightened by the terrible look in those eyes that had always been so full of laughter.

"'Don't you love me?' I whispered.

"'Didn't I show you how I loved you by sparing your life? Didn't I prove my love by coming to you in this mortal guise? Have I ever given you reason to doubt my love when I held you in my arms, cared for your house, and bore you a daughter? So why now do you question my devotion?'

"I had nothing to say to that. So she donned her white kimono and left us.

"I have mourned her ever since. I hoped she would forgive me and return to us, but she never has. I was afraid to tell you her real name for fear she would take you away, leaving me alone. Now I am dying, and it doesn't matter anymore. Your mother's name is Yuki-hime-kami, the snow spirit."

The moment his mouth finished shaping those words, he drooped forward and died.

I wrapped his body in a blanket and laid him on his sleeping mat. My father had lived so long with a shattered heart. In all that time, had Mother even thought of us? Had she ever loved us?

I spoke her name.

"Mother! Yuki-hime-kami!" I cried. "Yuki-hime-kami! Yuki-hime-kami!"

The fire's light turned from orange-red to a cold, lifeless blue. It crackled and sang, not with the snap of burning wood, but with the sharpness of ice warmed by sunlight. White smoke gushed into the room from the chimney, and it was neither sooty nor hot, but cold, and smelled of the clean tang of fresh snow. She, my mother, stepped out of the smoke in her white kimono. While my father's face had become creased with age, and strands of gray mingled freely with darker locks, she had not aged. She was as beautiful, as young, as the day she had left.

"My daughter, you have grown up." She held her arms wide for an embrace, but I did not go into them.

"I am eighteen years old," I said. "Next week, I am to be wed to Roku."

She let her arms drop to her side. "You say that as though you spoke of a funeral and not your own wedding. Don't you love him?"

I was angry then. "Who are you to speak of love? Father loved you, and look what happened to him."

She gazed at my father's swaddled body, and a tear glittered in her eye. It fell and shattered on the floor, a droplet of ice. "I loved him, too, my handsome woodcutter. It is why I had to leave."

"What do you mean? You left because of some silly promise."

"I left to save his life. I am a snow spirit, Sekka. I am frigid death. I fell in love with your father, but by the laws of the winter gods, I had to kill him. So I hid and gave up my immortality, content in your father's love. But the moment he spoke of the night we met, the last night I was Yuki-hime-kami, the gods remembered me. I had to leave, or they would demand I kill him."

"Are you here to kill me now?" I asked.

"Of course not. You are half snow spirit, Sekka. You may come with me and live forever. I can show you winter caves where the sun dances from icicle to icicle, fragmenting into a rainbow prism; midnight pools, cold and deep, that shelter the bones of creatures so old, their memories are no more than half-remembered stories; and the perfect silence of a snow-covered cliffside, hovering on the verge of avalanche. These secrets I would share with you."

"And will you also teach me to kill men with my breath?"

"Yes." My mother had the decency to lower her eyes. "It is the price of immortality. We remain young and beautiful forever, free to go where we will, unrestrained by the laws of man. And truly, what else have you to look forward to? Growing withered and old, Roku's children growing in your belly, sucking away your life, in toil and hardship?"

I thought of Roku, with his silly, crooked mouth that quirked on one side when he laughed. And the way his eyes had been so eager and hopeful when he asked my father for my hand, lingering on my face for the smallest sign of encouragement. I thought of sitting at his hearth, listening to his voice telling me of his day as I mended a series of clothing—his, mine, our children's. And I imagined my hands growing gnarled and the light fading from my eyes as my children grew up around me.

"I choose life and love, Mother," I said. "For the price of immortality is more than murder, it is love. You cannot love."

My mother smiled. "You have chosen wisely, my daughter."

Whatever it was I had expected, it had not been her blessing.

She gazed at the stiffening shape of my father's body. "But in one thing you are wrong. I *can* love. I never stopped loving him."

I felt tears sear my eyes, and I was once again five years old. I went into her waiting arms, no longer chilly with cold, but warm and yielding. There was so much I wanted to tell her: awkward kisses in the forest with Roku, how the mere sound of my name from his lips made me smile with joy—all the vital moments of my life she had missed.

She pulled away, and it was just like the last time, thirteen years ago, when she had untangled herself from my arms. Except this time, she went to my father, instead of leaving him.

She lifted his body as though he were made of paper, or snowflakes. The door blew open, sending a spray of needle-sharp ice crystals flurrying inside. A winter storm, a blizzard, had sprung up as we talked. She carried him out into the whirling snow.

As the world grew formless and indistinct in the storm, I watched as she became mist, fading into the soft whiteness that poured out of the sky. My father's body in her arms faded with her.

Roku and I married and are happy together. We have ten plump children, and though all of them are fair like me, they are vibrant and alive, with the hearty laugh of their father.

I have no regrets, even though sometimes life has been hard. I have always had Roku standing beside me, and his warm arms hold me at night. He tells me every day how beautiful I am, even though my face is seamed with years and my back is bent.

But in winter, sometimes, when the fire blazes high and hot, I peer out through the patina of frost on the window. Occasionally, I think I can see two figures: a man, tall and proud, with a woodcutter's breadth of shoulder, dancing with a beautiful woman in a white kimono. And other times, all I can see is the whirl of snowflakes in the air.

I've been fascinated by the Japanese snow woman folktale from the first time I read it. I never considered Yuki-onna to be a monster but rather a tragic, lonely figure. Winter is harsh and uncompromising, hard to live with and hard to love, but maybe

beneath the frosty demeanor, there's a heart longing for warmth and passion. Or maybe, having grown up with brutal Midwestern winters, I've finally come to grips with my unresolved issues about the cold.

The Tanuki-Kettle

When Hisa was a baby, her mother called in a soothsayer to cast her daughter's horoscope. The old woman pulled out her astrology charts and consulted them while incense turned the air blue with perfumed smoke. That day, the fortuneteller had a headache and was in a black mood. Though Hisa's mother brought her a cup of hot, green tea and fanned her sweating brow, the old woman continued to scowl.

"This child will be too bold for her own good," the fortuneteller grumbled.

"Is there nothing I can do?" asked Hisa's distraught mother. "I could hire tutors to teach her the folly of brashness."

"That is not sufficient." The soothsayer's eyes lit upon the brimming teapot. "She must grow up to be a lowly tea girl."

Hisa's mother wanted, above all, for her daughter to have a joyful and serene life, as befitting a devout follower of Buddha. Did not the teachings of Buddha extol the virtues of poverty and humility? Hisa's mother bowed her head to fate. If the cosmos wished her daughter to be a tea girl, so be it. She bundled Hisa in the poorest swaddling she could find, purchased a teahouse in a humble village, and took up residence there. She raised her daughter to be thoughtful and kind, and above all to understand that every moment presents an opportunity to act, and that these choices determine one's happiness.

When Hisa's mother caught the lung cough and passed on to her next life, Hisa took charge of the teahouse. When a new landowner moved into the village and raised everyone's taxes, she accepted it with philosophic grace. She did, however, wish the new landowner, Lord Shuichi, would be more considerate. He brought his hunting parties thundering through the narrow streets of the village at all hours, day and night, whooping fit to awaken the ancestral spirits. The rumble of hoofs knocked shelves awry on the walls, and pots and pans free from their hooks.

One dawn, when Hisa was preparing for her busy day, Lord Shuichi took his hunters racing past in the street outside the teahouse. Their commotion startled Hisa so much that she dropped the copper kettle she was scouring. A great gash appeared in the lid as the kettle bumped and rolled over the hard, stone floor.

"Oh, pickled plums!" Hisa exclaimed. As everyone knew, an imperfect teakettle brewed imperfect tea. She examined the rent in the metal. It was quite wide.

Hisa glowered. Enough was enough. She would petition Lord Shuichi to cease the thoughtless ruckus and to compensate her for her loss.

As she opened the door, Hisa was surprised to see an iron kettle sitting on her step. It had a large, round belly and four stumpy legs. The spout was wide and curved like a fox's mouth with two round, black eyes above it. And most curious, a pair of pointed triangles jutted from the top, exactly like a pair of ears.

"What an unusual teakettle." Hisa looked, but there was no one about.

She set aside her broken pot and brought the new, iron one inside. She poured sweet, cool water into it. Where her old kettle took eight dippers of water, this new one required a full twelve to fill.

Hisa stoked the fire high and lifted the kettle to the hook.

"Mistress, I thank you for the drink, but please don't put me on the fire."

Hisa spun around, sloshing water on the floor. "Who said that?"

"It was I, mistress. The teakettle."

Hisa stared at the iron pot in her hands. "Teakettles do not talk."

"I'm only pretending to be a teakettle."

"What are you when you're not frightening tea girls? A *tengu* demon, perhaps?"

"Oh no. Nothing like that. I'm just a *tanuki*."

Hisa laughed. "A raccoon dog? My new teakettle is a raccoon dog? How on earth did you end up like this?"

"Well, mistress, a teakettle is round with a large belly, and so are tanuki, so it seemed an easy shape to take. I was in a hurry, you see."

With gentle consideration, Hisa set the tanuki-kettle down. "But why did you need to change shape?"

"Ah." The tanuki-kettle seemed to droop. The high ears sagged, and the muzzle bowed, spilling a trickle of water. "I was chasing chickens in the lord's courtyard. I only do it for sport, you understand. I didn't mean any harm. But Lord Shuichi did not find my choice of recreation amusing. He assembled his hunters to chase me. In order to escape, I changed my shape. Tanuki are quite good at that. But please, good mistress, don't put me on the stove. It's very hot, and I'll be burned."

Hisa giggled at the tanuki-kettle's anxious tone. "How will I make tea, then? Besides, you should not chase chickens. It distresses them, and does not the Buddha teach us to cause no suffering? Do you not think it fitting to suffer my cook fire as reparation for your naughty deed?"

"Oh, please, mistress!"

"I'm teasing you, Tanuki. Of course I won't put you on

the stove." She retrieved her copper kettle. "I can use this one. I will simply have to tell my patrons what happened and charge them half my usual fee." She poured water into the broken kettle and set it on the fire.

The tanuki-kettle shuddered.

"Why don't you turn back into a tanuki, if the fire troubles you so?" asked Hisa.

"I can't. I can only change my shape at night. While the sun promenades in the sky, I'm stuck in whatever form I took when the cock crowed."

Hisa covered her smile with her hand, not wishing to offend the tanuki-kettle. "Is it so terrible being a teakettle?"

"I cannot run or jump, mistress. And I have a fearsome itch behind my left ear."

Hisa, struggling to maintain a solemn expression, scrubbed behind the teakettle's ears. "Is that better?"

The tanuki-kettle sighed. "May good fortune be yours forever, mistress."

Steam began to billow in clouds and streamers from the torn copper lid on the stove. Hisa scritched the tanuki-kettle one last time before lifting the hot copper kettle and pouring boiling water into serving pots filled with tea leaves.

Swirling a sip into a cup, she tasted it. "Bitter, as I feared," Hisa said. "I hope my customers will be charitable." She set the pots on a tray.

"Wait, mistress. I can help."

"You are volunteering to go on the fire?"

The tanuki humphed, and its mouth seamed shut.

Hisa was instantly contrite. "I'm sorry for teasing you. Please tell me how you can help."

"I have already done it."

"What?"

"I'm not telling, but you will thank me later."

The tanuki-kettle refused to speak another word, no matter how Hisa cajoled and wheedled. She even scrubbed its iron ear again, and although one eye fluttered closed in pleasure, not a single word passed through its spout.

"I cannot spend my morning beseeching a kettle," Hisa said at last. She picked up her tray and went out to her thirsty customers.

First was Kisho, the fisherman.

"I'm very sorry," Hisa said. "My teakettle broke this morning, so the tea is bitter. But to make up for it, I will only charge you half price."

Kisho, who was not known for his cheerful disposition, frowned and accepted the cup she offered. He took a cautious sip, and a magnificent smile spread over his face.

"That is quite a joke you played, Hisa! To make me expect bitter tea and then to serve me this kingly silver leaf!" He slipped several *shu* on her tray, double the usual charge. "Keep it coming, eh?"

Perplexed, Hisa went over to Ryo, the tailor, and Haru, the goatkeeper. She served them tea with her apologies, and again, they, too, exclaimed it was the best, sweetest, and most delicious tea they had ever had. Haru gave her an extra *shu*, and Ryo, not to be outdone, gave her two extra.

Hisa skipped back into the kitchen. "Tanuki-kettle! Whatever it was you did, thank you!" And she kissed the kettle on its cool, iron ear.

"I told you, you'd thank me." Despite the satisfied words, the tanuki-kettle sounded shy. For a moment, the gray iron took on a faint, pinkish cast.

Hisa wanted to stay and question the tanuki-kettle, but her customers clamored for her. At the end of the morning, her face flushed from running to and fro and her apron pockets bulging with money, Hisa plopped down in the kitchen.

"Goodness. I don't think I've ever had such a busy day. It seems everyone from the cart drivers to the silk weavers came in to sample your tea!"

The tanuki-kettle regarded her with shining eyes. "Hisa,

have you ever wanted to be other than a humble tea girl? I have a little magic—"

Hisa patted the tanuki-kettle on its round belly. "Do not squander more miracles on me. I am perfectly happy. I would not wish my life otherwise."

"Is there nothing you desire?"

Hisa paused. "Well, I confess I am lonely sometimes, but that is not something tanuki magic can fix."

Just then, the little chime over the teahouse door rang, announcing the arrival of customers. Hisa picked up her tray and ran out to greet them. She didn't have a moment to catch her breath until the sun had turned away to allow Lady Moon to unveil her face. When she returned to the kitchen, the tanuki-kettle was gone.

"Ah, my friend," Hisa said. "I would like to have seen you in your natural shape. I hope you are jumping, running, and scratching to your heart's joy."

Exhausted, Hisa lay down on her tatami mat and closed her eyes.

She was awakened by the rumble of hoofs. The vibrations grew so fierce, her broken copper kettle fell off its shelf and cracked its base.

"Scorched rice cakes!" Hisa cried. "Now it can't even hold water!"

She stalked to the door and flung it open. Lord Shuichi *would* hear her grievance. Before she could take a step, a flurry of russet fur streaked at her.

"Mistress, mistress, save me!"

Hisa recognized the tanuki's voice and spread wide her arms. The raccoon dog sprang, and as it hurtled through the air, its four legs stiffened. Its coat became sleek and hard, and its tail fused to its back.

"Oof." Hisa caught the tanuki-kettle in her arms and staggered back.

"Miss! You! Tea girl!"

With her arms wrapped around the kettle, Hisa turned. It was not the landowner who led the hunt, but his son, Akio. His face was angry and red as he swung off his horse.

"Give me that tanuki," he demanded. "It has been terrorizing my father's chickens."

Hisa raised an eyebrow. "This is a teakettle. Teakettles do not chase chickens." She jabbed the tanuki-kettle with a stern finger. "Do they?"

The tanuki-kettle uttered a tiny, apologetic whimper.

"It is a magical raccoon dog," the landowner's son said. "It can change shape."

"What silliness. It is my new teakettle. I had to acquire a new one because you and your gang of ruffians," and she waved her hand at Akio, "keep charging up and down the street when decent people are trying to sleep or make a living! Because of you, I dropped my old copper kettle yesterday, and the lid broke."

Hisa shook her finger, and the landowner's son, taken aback, retreated.

"Then, this morning," Hisa continued, "your din caused my already-broken kettle to fall off the shelf and crack so it can no longer hold water."

Akio fell back another step.

"And now you want to steal my new kettle?"

Akio's eyes grew wide as plates. "I–I did not realize—"

"Of course you didn't. All you care about is galloping about, chasing helpless raccoon dogs! And when you cannot catch them, you turn on innocent teakettles!"

The tanuki-kettle squirmed guiltily in her arms. Hisa thumped it with her finger, and it stilled.

"Let me make amends," said Akio. "I did not realize the huntsmen were such a nuisance."

Hisa, who had expected argument and blustering, stopped short. "You're apologizing?"

"The Buddha has expounded on the importance of

reflecting before, during, and after performing an action. Since I have neglected to reflect before and during my actions, it behooves me to at least consider them afterward."

Until that moment, Hisa had not noticed how Akio's eyes sparkled with intelligence and good humor, nor how strong and straight he stood.

"The Buddha is wise," she agreed. "Would you like to discuss this over tea?"

Akio bowed. "I would be honored."

Of course, when Hisa realized she needed to heat water and the only kettle was the tanuki, she hesitated. "Actually, I have not, um, properly tempered this kettle. Would you care for some rice wine instead?"

Akio grinned. "It is far too early for wine. Come, this is a teahouse. Let us have tea."

Hisa had no intention of setting the poor tanuki on the stove, but at the same time, if she didn't, Akio would surely wonder. She glanced down to see the tanuki-kettle close one eye in a conspiratorial wink. The next moment, a tendril of fragrant steam issued from the spout.

Hisa felt a grin tugging her lips. To hide it, she turned away to set a pair of cups on a tray and poured a stream of the most delicate, perfumed chrysanthemum tea.

Akio took a sip. His face softened into lines of delight. "This is most wondrous tea."

Hisa lowered her eyes modestly and sipped. Indeed it was delicious, the finest tea she had ever tasted.

"Any tanuki, or tanuki-kettle, that can brew such wonderful tea can chase my father's chickens whenever it likes." Akio bent low so he was eye to eye with the tanuki-kettle. "Although it would probably be best if such a tanuki restrained itself to times when my father was not at home."

The tanuki-kettle blushed. "I'm sorry, master. I promised Hisa I would leave your chickens alone, for the Buddha frowns upon such indulgence. But it was the only way I could think of you meeting her."

Akio choked on his tea. When he had finished coughing (and after Hisa had thumped him several times on the back), he stared at the tanuki-kettle.

"It spoke!"

"Of course it spoke." Hisa poured herself another cup of tea. "It is not a rude tanuki-kettle, just a mischievous one."

Akio began to chuckle. His chuckles turned to guffaws. Soon his laughter belled throughout the teahouse.

"I have never met as bold and interesting a person as you, Hisa," he said, wiping tears of merriment from his eyes. "May I visit you again?"

Hisa felt her heart somersault in her chest. "Of course."

Akio called on Hisa every day. He made sure the huntsmen stopped shouting and galloping through the streets and he also cautioned them to never, ever harm a tanuki. The tanuki, for his part, stopped distressing the chickens.

In good time, Hisa asked Akio if he would like to wed her. Akio, who had been waiting for just the right moment to propose, agreed—when he could find his voice again. At their wedding, instead of sake, they served the most superb tea anyone had ever tasted. And if the guests noticed the teakettle winking or spilling tea as it whispered to the bride or groom, they were too polite to comment.

"The Tanuki-Kettle" was inspired by classic Japanese "Bunbuku Chagama" or "Lucky Teakettle" folktales and also my pet skunk, Hobkin—although the tanuki here is more courteous and better spoken than Hobkin. Tanuki, like foxes, have a traditional role in Japanese folklore. They are depicted as mischief-makers and shape changers who can be both troublesome and helpful. Originally mistaken by the Japanese to

be badgers or raccoons, the tanuki is actually neither; it is an unusual species of dog. I've scoured the stores, both brick-and-mortar and Internet, for a tanuki teakettle, but so far, I haven't found one. Haven't been able to find a skunk teakettle, either.

Honor is a Game Mortals Play

Grandfather wished I had been a boy. He never spoke of it when he lived, but it was the same as when I scorched the rice porridge, or when I came home with the traps empty and dangling in my hands; the silent disappointment shone clear in his eyes. Now that he was dead, I didn't have to bear the heaviness of his frown or the disapproving shake of his head, but that brought no surcease.

His ghost whispered in my ear, poisonous words that had no place in a harmonious household.

"Ayame, your tears are as welcome to me as a drunkard's spittle," his ghost hissed. "What a sniveling weakling you have become."

The hem of my mourning-white kimono lifted, brushed by fingers of heat from Grandfather's funeral pyre. The ash spun into the air, stinging my face and blinding me, as a counterpoint to the ghostly tirade.

I didn't think less of Grandfather for his ghost's cruel outburst. The dead, after all, were renowned for their lack of decorum.

"I did not cry when your father left, dishonoring me with

his defiance," his spirit continued. "Nor did I shed a tear when he returned destitute and sick with a baby in tow, or even when he died, leaving only a granddaughter to carry on my legacy. And now you weep at my funeral?"

Grandfather had reared and sheltered me, even named me. He had taught me to respect and understand the harmony of the cosmos, shown me how each tree, rock, and creature was an exquisite miracle, playing its individual melody in the great symphony of the universe. The words of an angry *yurei*, the manifestation of his unnatural death, would not change sixteen years of respect and love. But they did stem my tears.

"While my father chose to walk another path," I said, "my steps will follow yours, Grandfather. I will purge his dishonor."

I heard the clack of phantom teeth. "Honor! As though a girl could understand honor."

I bowed my head and intoned a prayer, one to mollify a newly dead spirit.

"Spare me your pious gibberish," Grandfather's *yurei* snarled. "I taught you those sacraments, spoke them at temples and altars before you were born."

"If my prayers are not to your taste, should I begin the *tsuina* ceremony?" I asked. "Have you become a hateful poltergeist, an *ara-mi-tama* that I must exorcise?"

"Disgraceful, wicked girl. You dare to threaten me? Do you think because you are my kin that I will not curse you?"

"Peace, Grandfather. I know my duty. I will slay the demon that murdered you. I swear upon the flames of your pyre and the ashes of your body that I shall avenge you. It will be my first act as a *taijiya*, my first demon hunt."

The *yurei* was silent for the space of several heartbeats. I wiped the tears and ashes from my cheeks with a corner of my sleeve and gazed clear-eyed into the dying flames.

"Very well," he said at last. "Honor your oath and I'll not trouble you again. But should you bring further shame upon this family, I will visit upon you all the horrors that are at the disposal of the dead."

"I will not fail."

"Then finish this. I am done."

I bowed to the now-embers of Grandfather's pyre and tossed handfuls of parched beans to the four corners of the world.

"Depart! Depart!" I called to the north and the east. "Depart," I cried to the south.

When I turned to the west, out of the edge of my eye, I saw a glimmering blue light rise from Grandfather's funeral altar. It flew into the sky, chasing after the last tendrils of smoke.

"Depart, Grandfather," I whispered. "The serenity you crave awaits you in the Pure Land."

I turned my back on the smoldering remains of what had been a magnificent bonfire and climbed the familiar path that led to the hut where I had grown up.

Without Grandfather, those walls no longer shaped my home. I wondered if that made the entirety of the world my home, for nothingness and fullness were but two sides of completeness.

I smiled at the thought. It was the sort of puzzle Grandfather might have posed. The notion buoyed me as I removed my mourning garments, folding the white kimono into a neat square and setting it atop Grandfather's rolled-up sleeping mat. But when I made to don Grandfather's red kimono, the badge and uniform of a demon queller, I felt the burden of my uncertainty return. I set the kimono aside and slipped into my comfortable, colorless *yukata* instead. Tomorrow would be soon enough to garb myself in red.

I knelt before our tiny house altar. Tomorrow I must slay the demon that had stricken Grandfather with the freezing sickness, a demon powerful enough to overcome an experienced *taijiya*. And despite his wrinkles and gray hairs, Grandfather had been strong enough to carry two stone cauldrons upon his shoulders.

Grandfather's *yurei* had been right. I was frightened and unsure, a banquet of weakness for hungry ghosts and demons to feast upon. And now I was alone, without anyone to rescue me should I falter. I beseeched any benevolent kami deigning to listen for strength and wisdom.

My meditations complete, I curled upon my straw mat and clenched shut my eyes. Though my head was empty, sleep was as elusive as a single minnow in a burbling stream.

At the first glint of dawn's banner, I rose, no wiser or stronger, and significantly less rested. And I still could not bear to clothe myself in Grandfather's red kimono. I draped my *yukata* about my shoulders once more and tucked a rice cake into its worn sleeve, bundling a wooden bowl and chopsticks alongside it. I tied a pot of sake to my simple, unadorned obi, and got Grandfather's satchel from the hook where it always rested. Slipping his red uniform to the bottom, I filled the rest with the tools and weapons of the *taijiya*: a rustling packet of carefully inscribed spells, vials of herbs, and bottles of ointments. At last, I took up Grandfather's *shakujou*, a stout oak staff carved with holy blessings. It contained a core of iron, and two golden pins protruded like horns from its knotted crown.

Packed and provisioned, I turned my sandals to the west, for that had been the direction I'd seen Grandfather's spirit go when it released its hold.

As I journeyed, I scanned the skies and studied the trees for signs of the demon's passage. Such a strong evil couldn't have passed without leaving certain indications, fluctuations of energy like footprints in the mud.

The forest's ki nudged me to the base of a spreading maple tree. I fingered a single red leaf, crisped with rime, on an otherwise verdant branch.

A rustling in the underbrush caused me to spin about, gripping the *shakujou* in both hands.

A russet face with a pointed muzzle and shining eyes

regarded me from the knots of a bristly hawthorn bush. The creature stepped from her shelter, nimble as a cat, and waved a dark brush of tail in greeting—a fox.

I exhaled my relief.

"Hai!" she called. "Are you responsible for the chill in the air? If so, please desist. I haven't been able to catch anything to eat all morning."

"It's not my doing," I said, "but perhaps I can ease your empty belly." I offered her a corner of rice cake.

The fox eyed the morsel. "I'm sure that's tasty, but don't you have anything stronger, something to chase away the cold? I can barely feel my nose."

It was unwise to displease a fox, so I splashed some sake into my wooden bowl and set it down.

"That's more like it!" She lapped the wine, licking her whiskers to catch the last drops. "For your generosity, here's some friendly advice: Turn back. There's trouble ahead."

I bowed. "I hope you don't think me ungrateful, but I regret I'm honor bound to press on."

"Oh? Well anyway, that's hardly an even trade, advice being free and not worth a drop of sake. I'll give you another bit of counsel: Stay on the path. Don't vary your course."

I frowned. "Both turn back and go forward?"

The fox grinned, her tongue lolling from her muzzle. "If your yang is nourished and your yin starved, does that make you happy or miserable? Besides, what sort of advice do you expect a mouthful of sake to get you?" She barked, the fox equivalent of laughter, and bounded away.

I shook my head. Foxes. I would rather face a *tengu* demon than a friendly fox. With their riddles and pranks, they might ruin you even as they tried to help. At least with a *tengu*, you always knew what its teeth meant.

A puddle of ice-crusted mud caught my eye. It was a thick crimson. Over it, a copper tang hung like a shroud in the air. Several steps away, tiny red berries ornamented a young lilac tree—wet fruit that thawed into droplets of blood. A bloody icicle hung suspended from a twig like a red needle.

Perhaps because of my agitation from encountering the fox, I did not notice the man lying beneath it until he groaned.

In my defense, his kimono was dark—a chestnut brown with bands of deep ginger that blended into the crisscross shadows beneath the arching canopy. His hair also camouflaged him, a torrent of black that rooted him among the moldering verdure on the forest's floor. Still, his skin was whiter than milk, white as mourning. I should have seen him.

He watched me through half-lidded eyes. The source of the metallic bouquet suffusing the air was the seeping gash in his side. Even felled and half-conscious, I was struck by his beauty—the aristocratic lines of his face and the grace of his limbs. I'd never before seen such a nobly formed man.

When I stepped closer, he raised his arm, and I saw the weapon gripped in his fist, a katana of folded steel, a samurai's sword.

"Come to finish me off, witch?" His voice was silver silk, frayed with pain. "Or merely to watch me die?" The katana wavered. How long had he lain there, bleeding in the dirt?

"I mean you no harm," I said.

He squinted. "What game are you playing now, Yuki-onna? How like you to turn my final moments into some farce." His words grew indistinct. "It's not a very good disguise in any case." His head drooped, and his arm slipped to his side, although he continued to cling to the katana.

I crept nearer and kneeled, counting upon his weakness to keep him from chopping me to bits. The icy mire of blood and soil soaked into my *yukata*.

I set the *shakujou* aside so I could open his kimono, noting as I did its sleek softness—not wool or even felt— luxurious as fur but thin as silk. His skin burned fever hot save for the bubbling hole—from a dart or arrow, perhaps—that poured frozen mist into the air. Whatever the cause of his injury, it was feeding upon his body's warmth, his vital ki. It wouldn't be enough to staunch the bleeding; I had to neutralize that poisonous cold or it would kill him.

I drew one of the pins from Grandfather's *shakujou*. I disliked these slim implements, so finely honed it seemed every time I handled one, I must pay for the privilege with blood. Grandfather had often despaired at my clumsiness, sighing as he wrapped my gold-scored fingers in linen. But they were thrice blessed and inscribed with prayers—*taijiya* tools to negate demon magic.

Moving fast as thought, the man snatched my wrist. I flinched, and the edge of his katana hovered at my throat.

"You're not *her*," he growled. "Did she send you to torment me?"

I spoke softly, as though to a frightened animal. "The dart that wounded you carried a curse, and I believe the point is still embedded." I tilted the sliver of gold so a wisp of sunlight could highlight the prayers etched along its length. "This is a *gofu*, a blessed amulet to counteract demon energy."

He studied me, his eyes creased with pain. "Not that," he rasped. "Use my *shoto* to dig it out."

"But—"

"Else plunge that thorn into my heart and have done with it." He closed his eyes and released me.

There was only one reason a creature would refuse the touch of a holy charm. I leaned close, searching. They had been concealed by the darkness of his hair and the lattice of shadows, the elegant pair of black horns that twisted from his temples.

I was a fool. Worse than a fool. This wasn't a hapless man but an *oni*, a malicious demon of brutal hungers. The drape of his kimono derided me, the tiger-stripe pattern evident now, clear indication of his true nature. I hovered in indecision, poised to drive the *gofu* into his heart as he'd suggested.

But he was so defenseless. And so beautiful. Compassion, what Grandfather had called the foundation of a *taijiya*'s art, and also something else, something I did not wish to admit to, wouldn't let me finish him.

Instead, I tucked the *gofu* into my obi and pulled the wooden chopsticks from my sleeve. I found the demon's *shoto* sheathed at his hip, a long knife of gleaming steel, sharp and deadly as spite. It sheered into his flesh as easily as slicing water.

His cooled blood spilled over my hand. The sinews in his throat tightened, bowing his head back, but he didn't cry out. I cut again, widening the entry in order to insert the tips of my chopsticks within. His silent anguish continued, and I suffered with him.

His breath juddered through clenched jaws as I probed, searching with both blunt wood and also with that other awareness, the thrumming along my nerves that alerted me to *youki*, demon energy.

I touched the knot of cold with a chopstick at the same moment as I felt it, a contamination like a drop of tar in white tallow. I gripped it with the chopsticks and tugged. It resisted, slick and lodged tight, requiring me to dig it free with wood and steel.

The *oni* suffered my ministrations in silence.

At last I saw a pale bead peeping from the edge of his wound. Frozen blood encased it in a growing block of red. It wedged there, fouling my attempts to pry it loose. Despite his fortitude, I could not subject the *oni* (or myself) to another incision, so I used my fingertips to pluck it out.

As soon as I touched it, the bead slid into my palm.

The *oni* went limp, a ragged sigh slipping from his lips.

A bolt of winter hammered my hand, a numbness that sliced through muscle and bone. I dropped the *shoto* and drew the *gofu* from my sash. I stabbed the cursed pellet, and it shattered beneath the golden tip like brittle ice.

I thought the *oni* had finally slipped the yoke of consciousness, but when I pulled a length of linen from my satchel, I saw the glimmer of his eyes beneath his lashes, watching me.

In a rush, I remembered tales of *oni* who lusted after human women, violating helpless maidens before devouring their flesh. Fear sped my pulse, and also an intriguing thrill that brought guilt rushing after. I gripped the *gofu* tighter. It nicked my thumb, drawing a thread of blood from tip to meaty pad.

I swore and dropped the razor-edged metal. I immediately scrabbled after it, sifting the dirt with my fingers for the splinter of gold. Only after I'd found it and shoved it back into the *shakujou* did I recall the *oni*.

The demon had not moved during my antics, although his lips now wore a curve of mirth. I busied myself with herbs and bandages.

"That's not necessary," he murmured.

I glared at him, a swathe of linen hanging from one hand. "After all that, you don't expect me to let you bleed to death, do you?"

His smile mocked me as I inspected his side. I dabbed away the now-warm blood and discovered only a pinprick seam.

In a fluid motion, lithe as a dancer, he stood, towering over me. I scrambled to my feet, clutching the *shakujou* to my chest.

"As I said. Unnecessary." He pulled his kimono closed and knotted it with an obi striped orange and black like a tiger's tail. With skillful ease, he slid his katana into its scabbard.

He bent to collect his *shoto* from where I'd dropped it. I watched, bemused, as he twirled it in one hand. Would he now slash my throat, tear at my flesh and drink my blood?

It seemed not.

He wiped it clean with a tiger-pelt sleeve and sheathed it. His kimono possessed an unusual quality. Where it had been discolored by blood, it now gleamed, dry and unsoiled. The filth from his *shoto* rained from it in a gray dust.

In comparison, I felt grubby and unkempt with my

yukata stained and damp, and my hair a tangled nest about my face.

"Do all *oni* heal as quickly as you?" I asked.

His eyes flitted to Grandfather's *shakujou.* "Not always," he said. "Some faster than others. That stick you're sporting has hewn down its share of *oni* by the look of it. The *taijiya* you stole it from is going to be eager to have it back."

"I didn't steal it," I said. "It's mine."

The *oni* arched an eyebrow. "Is it? Pardon my ignorance. I have not heard of a maiden *taijiya* so confident that she heals mortally wounded demons in order to defeat them in honorable battle."

I paled. "Are we to battle, then?"

He laughed, displaying straight, white teeth with only a suggestion of flesh-tearing serration. "Only if you demand it." He bowed, every line of his body distorting the salutation into a jest. "As you have saved me, I'm yours to command." His eyes—feral, tawny orbs like a tiger's—glinted a challenge. "What would you have of me?"

"I don't recall *oni* being so honorable," I said.

"May a demon not have honor? Would it suit you better if I fell upon you, slavering and rapacious?"

"Tell me your name," I demanded, doing my best to achieve Grandfather's authoritative boom. I straightened my shoulders.

"I'm called Ronin by those who care to address me." His amusement was obvious even without his muted laughter. As I feared, I sounded more like a puffed-up mouse squeaking at a wolf than a *taijiya*.

"What is your business here, and where is the demon who caused your hurt? I've a score to settle with him."

"Her. It was a woman's hand that threw the dart." Ronin's manner switched to bleak bitterness in the space of those words. "My mistress brooks no defiance and no failure, she of the frozen heart, cruel Yuki-onna." Ronin lifted his eyes to the white-rimmed mountains behind us.

His wistfulness filled me with misery, a heartsick desolation.

"It wasn't so great a thing she demanded. I've won legendary prizes for her, magnificent and precious, razed whole villages at her whimsy, but at this, I balked. All she required was a certain female infant, with the only obstacle an old monk, her grandfather."

I started. "A girl and her grandfather?"

Ronin scowled, returned from whatever reverie he'd fallen into. "I killed the old man. He was stronger than I expected, but in the end, even his ki succumbed to Yuki-onna's frozen death, delivered by the edge of my katana." His laughter was harsh, dripping with self-loathing. "But I could not bring myself to fetch her some brat and told her so."

"W–what was the girl's name?"

Ronin shrugged. "Ayame or Ayemi, perhaps."

I felt as though I'd swallowed a lead ball. "It was you," I gasped. "You're the demon that killed Grandfather!"

His eyes widened. Faster than any man could move, he sprang at me.

Rather than drawing a *gofu* or swinging the *shakujou* to ward him off, I screamed, cringing like a useless fool. I expected to feel his teeth at my throat, but he scooped me into his arms.

The earth fell away as he swept us aloft.

I struggled, but his arms were a cage of marble and steel.

"A baby." His words were strangely fierce. "An *infant* girl."

Waves of heat throbbed through the dual layers of our garments, smoldering hotter than an open forge. The *youki* energy of an *oni* is akin to the ki of fire. It made me lightheaded and weak; I would have fainted but for the *shakujou* between us, radiating a soothing counterpoint. As dizzy as I was, I still noted that Ronin didn't care to touch it, buffering his skin with his tiger pelt where it pressed against him.

"Put me d–down!" I forced the words through chattering teeth.

"I regret I cannot. My mistress requires your presence." He flew, eyes fixed upon the summit of the tallest mountain. In the space of three breaths, the air grew chilly and thin, and whirling snowflakes powdered the sky. I writhed, half frozen by the piercing cold, half baking against Ronin.

"S–so much for a demon's honor."

He glanced at me. "You think honor is a game exclusive to mortals?"

"You s–seemed to tire of it quickly enough."

"Don't assume you know all the rules of this game, little *taijiya*." The resignation and sorrow in his voice were ancient as the mountain above us.

With a stomach-lurching maneuver, he deflected a gust of frigid wind with his back, sheltering me from the worst of it.

"By all the eight million kami, don't do that," I gasped. "Unless you intend to deliver me dead from fright."

"The cold will kill you faster than any distress I could provide."

"I wouldn't depend on that," I chattered.

"I could fly better if you carried your *shakujou*. It's awkward, wedged between us."

Ronin wanted me to keep the best weapon I had against demonkind? Why? He gazed over my head, intent on our journey.

"Very well, release my arms."

He adjusted his hold, cradling me beneath my knees and shoulders, and allowed me to slide the *shakujou* free. I wrapped one arm around it, and with the other, I plucked out a *gofu*. Gripping it as tightly as I dared in my numb fingers, I leveled the point over his heart.

Ronin tilted his head to regard first me and then the gold skewer pressing into his kimono. "If you don't put that away, you're liable to cut yourself again," he said.

"I have sworn to kill you, demon."

"We're quite high," he remarked. "If you stick me, I may not be able to keep from dropping you." He swooped at the distant crags below to illustrate.

I wrenched my eyes from the speeding ground. "Death doubtless awaits me at your destination anyway."

"Then perhaps I should do this before you send us tumbling from the sky." I felt long fingers tangle in my hair as he bent his neck, bringing his lips to mine. At the touch of his mouth, an ember flared between us, electrifying and sharp. I inhaled in astonishment, taking the firestorm of his breath into my lungs. Ronin tasted of smoke and hot steel, warm rain and summer winds. His kiss chased away the chill of the frozen air and left me breathless. Through the tiger pelt kimono, I felt him trembling.

He buried his face in my hair, his lips brushing my ear. "Kami of fire and light." I could barely hear him over the screaming wind. He crushed me to him, so I could not think.

"Ayame, I will be yours," he said, "to kill as you wish. If you will not allow me *seppuku*, I swear I will kneel to a blow from your *shakujou* or open myself to the point of your *gofu*. Only free me first, little *taijiya*. Please, free me first."

I had no more than a moment to splutter in astonishment.

He loosed his hold, and I cried out, expecting to plummet through a mountain's span of empty air. But my descent was brief; I sank not through the ether, but into snow, up to my ankles. My shout petered out, ending as a confused yip.

We had alighted during his kiss, and I had been too preoccupied to notice.

He kneeled.

I gaped, baffled, until I realized his obeisance was not to me. I turned, slow as a dream.

Behind me, not five strides away, stood the most exquisite maiden I had ever seen. Her skin was an ice blue so luminous she glowed against the backdrop of winter white. A curtain of raven-black hair cascaded to the ground, stray locks billowing in glossy streamers about her head. She wore a silk kimono—moonlight embroidered with clouds—and her eyes were dark as forever. There was a familiarity to her loveliness, like a forgotten memory or a dream.

She didn't walk but rather drifted to us, bare feet passing over the snow.

"You dare to return?" At odds with her visage, her voice was a knife of ice. "Do you love me so much, my samurai, that death means nothing to you?"

"Death has never meant anything to me, Yuki-onna." Ronin's words released me from my paralysis. I blinked, my eyes dry and chilled from staring.

She glanced at me. "And who's this?"

"She is Ayame. You charged me to fetch her."

"What nonsense are you babbling? You think I'll forgive your transgressions with a trick? I told you to bring me a girl child, an infant, not a maiden full grown."

"Girl children become maidens, my lady."

Her brow furrowed. "Could it be?" The edge of her voice softened. "Sixteen thaws and sixteen freezes. I'd forgotten how time affects those who bow to its passage." She caught my chin in her slender fingers and forced me to meet her gaze. "Do you remember me, child?"

Her touch sent tendrils of ice through me. "M–my apologies, l–lady, no," I stammered.

"You're shivering. Come closer. Let me wrap you in my kimono." She undid the knot of her obi and opened it, sweeping me into her embrace.

"No!" Ronin's shout floated to me, as though from a great distance.

Pressed against her skin, a glacial storm buffeted me—body and ki—tearing at my confusion, my unhappiness, and my lingering grief, even as it chilled me through. The *shakujou* slipped from my benumbed fingers.

Dimly, I heard the hiss of a katana leaving its scabbard.

I craned my neck so I could peer over Yuki-onna's white shoulder. Ronin whirled in a lethal dance, his katana a blur. Around him, white claws and fangs had sprouted, mindless snow kami whose only purpose was butchery. I saw his face as he parried, desperate and frantic—not for himself, but for me.

"Ayame."

So simply, with my name, she had me. A white mist—snowflakes and rime—billowed from her lips. It engulfed me and swept away everything that anchored my ki to my body: anger, compassion, and the resolve acquired through years as Grandfather's apprentice.

My shivering stopped; the cold no longer troubled me.

The folds of her kimono parted, leaving behind a memory of white silk whispering along my skin.

"Am I dead?" I asked.

She laughed, a delicate peal of ice crystals. "No, child, you are awake. The last sixteen years, that was the dream."

I heard Ronin cry out. Glancing back, I saw snow kami strewn in glittering shreds. He staggered and fell to his knees, clutching his side where crimson ribbons spilled through his fingers.

Yuki-onna leaned close. "In sixteen years, have you never wondered about your mother?" she whispered. "About me?"

I forgot Ronin.

Broken pieces of a puzzle I had not comprehended fell together: Ronin mistaking me in the forest, Yuki-onna's inexplicable familiarity, and her motive for wanting me in the first place. The answer was in the line of our limbs, the arch of our brows, the shared curve of our mouths—if only I had known to look for it. She and I were forged from the same mold, mother and daughter.

"Let me share my secrets with you." Her voice was as mesmerizing as falling snow. "We shall explore frozen caverns where the bones of ancient animals lie glittering like jewels, and bathe in black pools, still as glass, that no man has ever seen. I'll weave you a kimono of spun pearls and teach you how to kill with a sigh. We'll rule the kami of blizzards and tempests, and you will never die."

"Never die—?"

"Never. Never suffer the ruin of old age. All you must do is discard that part of you which cleaves to time and the flimsy sentiments of mortality."

"I don't understand."

"Your name, daughter. Renounce Ayame, frail and filled with doubt, and become Yuki-onna."

"Grandfather gave me my name," I said. "I promised I wouldn't dishonor him."

"We are Women of the Snow!" Her voice rang over the mountaintop. "We are not bound by man or god!"

"Ayame, don't." Ronin had stumbled forward, but his way was barred by the *shakujou* lying between us. "It's not life she offers but eternal death, an existence of inviolate cold. Her heart is a frozen rock. I know this better than anyone."

"Enough!" Yuki-onna gestured and tiny darts flew from her outstretched fingers. They lodged in Ronin's chest with a sound like pattering hail. He crumpled without a sound, his blood a poem in the snow, red brushstrokes on white paper.

It was my voice that cried out, a wail of anguish. I would have run to him, but Yuki-onna caught me back with steely fingers on my shoulder.

"He's nothing," she hissed. "His kind hunger after the young and beautiful. Don't throw away eternity for love of him. No matter how tender or how devoted he seems, he will abandon you when you become stooped and gray."

Her touch extinguished the tantalizing yearning I'd felt from the moment I'd seen Ronin under the lilac tree. No longer anxious or conflicted, I could step aside and regard my feelings, like studying an insect caught in honey. It was a relief, a deliverance to be free of them. Such peace was surely worth the trifle of a name.

It was on my lips, a glowing coal I could spit out and be rid of. But the heat in my mouth reminded me of Ronin's kiss. If I cast away my name, a kiss would mean no more than a breeze through my hair.

I rolled my name on my tongue, reliving the brief thrill of Ronin's touch, the taste of his passion. Was death so terrible a price to pay for the likes of joy, for even the smallest chance of happiness? Death, after all, was nothing more than a change, the other side of living. Without it, there was no life, and no love.

I swallowed.

"Even if love is fleeting, Mother, I want it."

Her face didn't change, but her eyes flashed with displeasure. "Fool. Love and death are the same."

She exhaled, and a cloud of sleet surged forth. Needles of ice blinded me, while a deeper, penetrating cold clamped me in a vise; I couldn't breathe, couldn't move.

My hand convulsed, and a new pain speared my arm, a pain that blazed. The *gofu*, I'd forgotten it. Forever eager to bite me—protesting my demonic lineage?—its keen edges sliced my fingers, thawing frozen nerves.

Calling upon every trick of will Grandfather had taught me, I stabbed that golden tooth at the arctic center, winter's heart.

Yuki-onna shrieked. Her scream became a howling snowstorm rushing to the sky. I covered my ears, but still I heard it. The sleet dissipated, and through stinging eyes, I saw her reel, her kimono whipping about like the edge of a blizzard. My mother grew indistinct as her *youki* fragmented, fading at last into nothingness. Quelled.

Overhead, the mountainside shuddered, throwing off its mantle of snow. An avalanche poured down, inexorable and inescapable.

My last thought before the frozen weight struck was that

Yuki-onna was wrong. Love and death were not the same, even if knowing one meant embracing both.

"Ayame, get up." Grandfather prodded me with a stiff finger, as he did every morning to wake me.

"How can it be dawn already?" I groaned.

"There's no dawn in death's Shadow Realm. Stop lazing about. I'm on my way to the Pure Land, and I'm in a hurry."

Memory lashed me alert. "The avalanche. Ronin!"

Grandfather smirked. "Didn't take you long to find yourself a young man, I see."

"But he's an *oni*," I moaned.

"So what? Your mother's a Snow Woman." His jovial grin turned solemn. "Do not fear the inevitable; destiny is best greeted with open arms. I always feared what would happen when she came back, but I should've had more faith in you. Your father loved her and though she destroyed him, he never regretted loving her. He was wise, just not strong enough. You, Ayame, are strong enough. Now be wise."

"Grandfather—"

"Must go now. Bye-bye." He patted my head. "Go have many daughters so you may be as proud of them as I am of you."

Then he vanished, leaving me in darkness. Cold, wet darkness. Snow. I was buried in snow. Waves of heat rose beneath me in a fluttering pulse. I was slumped over Ronin, sideways and crumpled, but whole.

I groped about until I could tell which end of him was up and wriggled through compacted snow until I reached his head. *Do not fear the inevitable.* Could I at least have qualms about the uncertain, Grandfather?

Destiny or no, I did what I'd longed to from my first glimpse of Ronin. I kissed him.

At first there was nothing, and I was terrified he was

gone. But then he inhaled. Like a spark touching rice paper, we ignited. He clamped me to him with one arm and fed from me, fierce and desperate, as though he would crawl down my throat. The heat we'd kindled erupted into a conflagration. I was overwhelmed, lost. There'd be nothing left of me, my ki sundered to ash and gone.

I didn't care. I met him, adding more fuel to the blaze.

We became molten steel, liquid fire, shining and white.

It was Ronin who broke away. I opened my eyes to see that the mountainside of snow had melted in a clearing around us. Tiger eyes, tawny as a summer afternoon, studied me.

"I thought she'd finished me," he said.

I sat in a puddle of slush, feeling both shy and defiant. And cold. "Rather, I finished her," I said.

He knelt awkwardly. "Will you allow me *seppuku*, mistress?"

I stared, disbelieving. "I will not!"

"I see. You would rather kill me?"

I propelled myself to my feet. "I would rather you had a brain, but it seems I might as well wish for wings." He already looked dry and sleek, even kneeling in melting snow, while I felt like a sodden lump. A *shivering* sodden lump.

I turned to storm off, not counting upon the drift of snow heaped to my waist.

"What of your vow?" Ronin stood at my back, close enough to caress my neck with his words.

I spoke over my shoulder. "My mother killed my father, and through you, my grandfather. By ending her, I have avenged my family."

I endeavored to contain my shivering so he wouldn't notice, but my efforts were futile. He wrapped his arms around me and I swayed, lulled by the warmth of him.

"Then what would you have of me?" he asked.

I held myself rigid. "Nothing. If you want to go, go."

His lips brushed my ear. "What if I want to stay?"

"Why would you want that? I'm not a beautiful immortal. I'll get old and wrinkled. I'll probably get a hump."

He laughed, a silken cord through my hair. "So?" He spun me about. His face was solemn, although his eyes twinkled. "While you are indeed quite beautiful, it's neither your creamy skin nor your lithe body which entices me. It is your spirit, endless and ageless. The fiery taste of your ki as it blazes against mine is more potent than a hundred barrels of wine."

He tipped my face up and kissed me. When he raised his head, I wasn't the least bit cold.

"So, what would you have of me?" he murmured.

I gazed into the amber glow of his eyes. "You. Just you," I whispered.

"Little *taijiya*, didn't I just say? I'm yours. To walk by your side and sleep in your arms, even to help you quell demons—other demons—if you insist."

An abrupt and enormous sneeze rocked me on my heels. "A way off this frigid mountain would also be appreciated," I sniffled. "And unless that fox has stolen my satchel, there's a certain red kimono I'd like back. I think it'll fit me now."

"It is my honor to oblige you," Ronin said.

Then we were airborne. Despite his words, I knew it was not honor that cradled me, nor honor that held me so tenderly. Honor was just a game, and I had already won the prize.

I was invited to contribute a story to the DAW anthology Heroes in Training *by editor Jim Hines, and I decided to revisit the Yuki-onna folktale which I'd explored a couple years earlier with "The Snow Woman's Daughter." The result was "Honor is a Game Mortals Play." I'm pleased with how both stories turned out, although I view "Snow Woman's Daughter" as more of a classic fairy tale and "Honor" as something of an adventure-*

romance, more manga than mythology. Then again, I've always been clueless when it comes to defining or categorizing my work.

The Raven's Brocade

It was known in the village where Binbou lived that although Binbou was very poor, he often gave food and money to penniless widows and hungry beggars. Most people thought he was kind and generous, but his brothers often teased him, calling him softhearted and foolish. "How will you attract a wife without any money?" they asked him.

So Binbou knew they would mock him for bringing the sick raven into his house. But it was cold outside, the winter air biting with teeth of ice and snow, and the fire was warm inside. What harm was there in settling a cold bird by the hearth? The fire would not burn any less hot or less bright. Binbou also gave her some of the rice he had made for his dinner. After all, what harm was there in feeding her some? Surely, what she ate would not make a difference in the fullness of his own belly.

The raven was quite beautiful, so black it was as if she had taken a bit of the night sky and sewn it to her feathers. She was half-dead from the cold, but as she lay by the fire, fed grains of rice from Binbou's own chopsticks, she began to revive.

The next morning, she was gone. Binbou suspected she had slipped out the chink in his roof, following the wisps of smoke from the fire. He hoped she would be well.

Later that day, a knock sounded at his door.

When he opened it, a woman with glossy black hair that fell to her ankles stood before him. Her skin was paler than the whitest lilies, and her eyes gleamed like fine onyx.

"The matchmaker has sent me to be your wife," she said.

Her name was Karasu and Binbou loved her immediately. They married that day.

Binbou's brothers came to congratulate him on his marriage, but when they saw how beautiful Karasu was, their eyes grew sharp with envy.

"You will never keep her," they said. "Such a beautiful woman will want silks to parade in and sweetmeats to eat instead of rice. She will leave you for a rich man."

Binbou grew unhappy at their words and Karasu saw this. "Why are you sad, my husband?" she asked.

"Because we are poor," he replied. "You should have silks to match your soft skin and fine things to eat."

"I don't mind," Karasu said. But she saw Binbou was still unhappy, so she hung a screen across their room. "Very well. Let me see what I can do, but you must promise not to look."

Binbou was curious, but he trusted his wife, so he sat beside the fire and waited.

The next morning, Karasu emerged from behind the screen. Her eyes, once glittering and bright, were now haggard. Her step was heavy, and her hair had lost some of its sheen. But she held a marvelous brocade cloth in her hands. It was the night sky—blackness so full and deep that Binbou felt he could fall into it and never come out—with an intricate weave that hinted of glossy wings, summer breezes, and the promise of sunrise after a long, cold night.

"Sell this," Karasu said, "and we will have money."

So Binbou brought the wonderful cloth to market. A noblewoman snatched it up, paying his asking price without even trying to haggle. With the money, Binbou bought sweetmeats, spices, and a pair of silk slippers for Karasu, as well as a chicken to lay eggs, and a goat that delivered creamy milk.

When Binbou's brothers saw all his riches, they grew quite jealous. "Where did you get all that money?" they asked.

Binbou explained about Karasu's weaving.

"It sounds worrisome," they said, "very worrisome. Surely your wife is up to no good. Who knows what she was doing while you sat so foolishly on the other side of the screen."

"Nonsense," Binbou said, but he grew uneasy.

Karasu noticed Binbou was still unhappy. "Do we not have enough money, now, my husband?" she asked, tiredly.

"We could always use more," he replied.

"Very well, let me see what I can do. But you must promise not to look." And she stepped behind the screen.

Binbou's curiosity was too great. He crept across the floor, his heart pattering at every whisper of dust and sigh of wood.

Behind the screen, a raven labored at a tiny loom. He recognized her as the bird he had saved. But where before her plumage had been magnificent and glossy, she was now tattered and miserable looking. Her feathers were ragged, and there were great bald spots on her back and wings, as though a cruel hand had plucked her bare. As Binbou watched, the raven turned her head and pulled out a fine, large tail feather and wove it into the growing brocade. She was weaving her own feathers into the lustrous cloth.

Binbou gasped when he realized this, ashamed he had listened to his brothers' jealous words.

Karasu, for it was none other than she, heard him. In the space of an eye blink, the raven grew, her wings turning into arms and her feathers into a mantle of once-glossy hair.

"Oh, Binbou," she said, "for shame. We could have been happy together, but there can be no happiness in a house of broken promises and distrust." She raised her arms, and her hair swirled around her like a flight of birds. She rose into the air and streamed out of the smoke hole in the roof, never to be seen again.

All his life, Binbou kept the half-finished cloth that Karasu had woven. He slept beneath it on winter nights and dreamed of black wings and bright, onyx eyes.

"The Raven's Brocade" is a retelling of the Japanese folktale "Tsuru no Ongaeshi" or "The Crane's Gratitude." The bird-heroine in the original tends to be either a crane or a heron, but I wrote this one summer after watching the birds in my backyard. One bird in particular kept coming back, a raven, and the way the sunlight glinted from her wings was both beautiful and magical. Black is the new white.

Shim Chung the Lotus Queen

In ancient times in Korea, the land where the morning is born, there lived a maiden named Shim Chung. She was the daughter of a blind beggar, and although they were so poor they had to share a bowl of rice for supper, they were happy. Shim Chung accompanied her father as he went begging for alms, and everywhere they went, people complimented her on her beauty and gentle grace. Her father's only regret was that he could not see his daughter's face and so could not appreciate her loveliness.

One day, a generous man put an iron nyang coin in the old man's bowl. Father and daughter were overjoyed.

"Take this money," the old man said, "and buy a half bag of rice at the market."

"Aren't you coming with me, Father?"

"I shall stay here in case our luck should continue. Do not worry; I have my cane to guide me."

Shim Chung hurried away, her thoughts on how full their bellies would be that night.

While she was gone, her father heard voices, laughing and merry.

"Surely where there are high spirits, there will be munificence." He headed toward them, but no matter how quickly he walked, the voices seemed always ahead of him. He found himself disoriented and confused. Deciding that he should go back to the familiar road before he became lost, he turned around. But where he thought there should be solid ground was only air. Tumbling and rolling, he stumbled down a deep ravine until he splashed to a stop at the bottom of a muddy trench.

Soaking wet and weighted by the folds of his *hanbok*, he tried to climb out, but the way was slippery and steep.

"Curse my blindness! Now I am trapped in a ditch. Help! Help!"

The old man heard the drum of running feet. A voice called down, "I am a monk from the temple. Reach your cane up, and I will pull you out!"

Giddy with relief, the old man lifted his cane, and with much tugging and grunting, the monk helped him out of the ditch.

"Oh, thank you, holy one," the old man said. "I don't know what I would have done if you hadn't come by."

"Lord Buddha was with you. He made sure I heard your cries."

The old man scowled. "If he were with me, then he should have stopped me from falling in, or better yet, restored my sight."

"Perhaps he has been waiting for your prayers at the temple. If you were to make an offering, might he hear you?"

The old man snorted. "As you can see, I am a wealthy man. I was on my way with three hundred bags of rice to the temple just now."

The monk's voice was solemn. "Then I will await you and your gift."

"I was only joking, monk. Where would I get three hundred bags of rice?"

But the monk did not reply. "Monk? Where did you go?"

The old man called and called, but there was only silence. He reached with his cane, and it tapped the solid dirt of the road, and there, the tree stump and familiar boulder where they begged for alms. He was where Shim Chung had left him. If not for his dripping *hanbok*, he would have thought he had dreamed his adventure.

Quite unnerved, he made his way home. Shim Chung was already waiting for him with a full pot of rice bubbling on the fire.

"Father! You're muddy and soaked through!"

The old man told her of the monk who had rescued him. "And the strangest thing was how I found myself back."

Shim Chung was quiet. "Father," she said, "I think you had a holy messenger visit you. He told you your sight would be restored if you presented three hundred bags of rice to the temple."

The old man's spirits leaped, then plummeted. "It is impossible. We cannot afford three bowls of rice, much less three hundred bags."

They ate their dinner in silence, the old man in despair and Shim Chung in contemplation.

Surely, Shim Chung thought, *Lord Buddha would not propose such a miracle if there was no hope.* She waited until her father began snoring on his sleeping mat. Quieter than a whisper, she donned her sandals and slipped out into the night. The moon was a gleaming lantern in the sky, lighting the path before her with a silver radiance. Shim Chung let the moonlight lead her steps. They guided her to a ship where a forlorn merchant captain gazed over the black waves.

"Good evening, sir," Shim Chung said. "Why do you look so sad on this beautiful night?"

The captain was surprised to see a lovely maiden before him. Her eyes reflected the dancing stars above.

"The Dragon King of the Sea is displeased with me," he said. "Every ship I have sent across his domain has been sunk by storms. When I went to consult the monks at the temple, they told me I must sacrifice a willing maiden to the ocean in order to appease him, or all of my ships will be forever doomed."

Shim Chung understood then what her fate must be. "What would you give to find such a maid?" she asked.

"Why, half my fortune, more even. For if I cannot sail, then surely I will lose all of it."

"I do not require half your fortune," she said. "Merely three hundred bags of rice. If you offer that to the temple in the name of my blind father, I will be your sacrifice."

The captain stared at the maiden, her face as clear and sweet as the dawn. "It will mean your death."

"To give my father sight, I would gladly die."

"If you are intent upon this course of action, then we sail tomorrow on the evening tide."

"I will meet you at the temple."

As Shim Chung returned home, her steps were light when she thought of how wonderful it would be for her father to see, but her heart was filled with worry. Who would care for him when she was gone?

The next morning, Shim Chung scrubbed their hut from roof to floor and mended all the rents in the rice paper shutters. When her father woke up, she had his breakfast porridge and tea ready for him.

"Father, last night I found a way to obtain three hundred bags of rice."

The old man dropped his chopsticks in surprise.

Shim Chung could not bear to tell him the truth, so she spun a lie. "A merchant captain is hiring me to clean his ship and cook for him."

"You have sold yourself into servitude? I cannot allow you to go! The sea is treacherous, and those who travel her are rough, uncouth men."

"It is already agreed upon. Do not be angry. I am happy, knowing that my labors will allow you to see."

The old man pleaded and shouted, but Shim Chung remained resolute. At last, he allowed her to lead him to the temple. There, as good as his word, the captain awaited them with three hundred bags of rice.

When father and daughter arrived, he bowed to the old man. "You have a virtuous and honorable daughter. I swear that she will be well treated on my ship."

Shim Chung gestured at him to cease talking, but the captain did not pay heed.

"It demonstrates rare courage that she would willingly sacrifice herself to the Dragon King."

"What?" The old man roared. "She said she was to clean and cook for you. I will not permit this!"

Shim Chung rested her hand on her father's arm while he shook with rage and fear. "Father, it is my destiny. Do not be sad, but rejoice that I embrace it."

She kissed her father and gently dislodged his hand from her wrist. It was the hardest thing she had ever done, turning her back on the sounds of her father's sobs of grief. They lingered long in her ears.

⁂

When she boarded his ship, the captain gave Shim Chung the finest silk robes to wear, as befitting a bride for the Dragon King, and offered her the choicest delicacies to eat. The crew were reverent and courteous as well, for they knew this maiden was their salvation.

Though they set sail on a sea calm and smooth, as soon as the shore disappeared from sight, the Dragon King began to thrash. The ship on his back was tossed like a beetle in a thunderstorm.

"It is time," Shim Chung said.

The captain looked into her brave face, and his heart turned leaden with remorse. "We could still turn back."

"No, the Dragon King wants his sacrifice." Shim Chung stepped to the deck. The rain lashed her, and the wind pushed her like a jealous bully. Calloused hands reached out to steady and guide her to the rail, though not a single crewman would meet her eyes.

Shim Chung gazed down at the frothing darkness and tasted salt on her lips—the ocean spray mixed with her tears. Before her courage could fail, she leaped in. The water closed over her head, and immediately the winds stilled and the waves quieted.

She was swept away by the freezing current, but instead of death greeting her, a pair of scarlet carp swam up. To her surprise, Shim Chung found she could breathe the water as easily as air. Her escorts brought her to a city of coral and pearl where the walls glimmered with light so that day was brought to the ocean's abyss.

There the Dragon King awaited her. Taking the guise of a man, he wore a living robe of brown seaweed and kelp, dusted by strands of coral. A crown of pearls encircled his brow.

"Shim Chung, is it of your own will that you have given yourself to my realm?" he asked.

"I thought it was to death that I gave myself. So yes, to restore my father's sight, I have come here gladly."

The Dragon King was delighted by the maiden's selflessness. "Then be welcome. In my city, you will live forever and want for nothing."

He had his servants twine strands of sea jade through her hair, and he presented her with bracelets and necklaces made from filigree shells as delicate as lace. He showed her the wonders of his seaweed gardens where sea horses sported with fish that flashed like opals.

But even though his kingdom was marvelous and the Dragon King was kind, Shim Chung was sad. As the weeks and months passed, she yearned for the blaze of sunlight on her face, and more, she missed her father. Though she never spoke of her sorrow, unhappiness dimmed her eyes, and she seemed to forget how to smile.

The Dragon King could not bear to be the cause of Shim Chung's misery, so he sent her back to the surface world, protected by the petals of a creamy lotus blossom. There she slept, serene and safe, floating to the shore.

The giant lotus was discovered by a king, who was fascinated by the beautiful flower. He had it brought into his palace in a basin of water, surrounded by silk tapestries and flickering lanterns. As the golden light lit the petals, the silhouette of a maiden's figure—slender and graceful—could be seen within.

Shim Chung yawned, stretched, and stepped forth. She was dressed like an empress—the Dragon King's last gift—in a red dress crusted in pearls with a tiara of white jade on her head.

"You are the loveliest thing I have ever seen," the king said. "Will you marry me and be my queen?"

The king's face held the peace of the ocean and his voice the warmth of the sun. Shim Chung blushed pink as the delicate core of a conch shell. "I will gladly marry you if you will allow my old father to live with us," she said.

"Of course."

As a wedding present, the king built a white carriage made of lacquered teak, carved into the shape of a lotus. He traveled with his bride to the hut she grew up in to take her father back to the palace.

When Shim Chung entered the humble structure, she expected to find her father with his eyes clear and bright. Instead, he sat in darkness with the fire unlit and his face turned to the wall.

Shim Chung ran to embrace him. "Father, why is it so cold in here? And why are you so thin?"

For a moment, it seemed the old man did not hear her, but then his face grew radiant with hope. "Is that Shim Chung? Have you returned to me as a ghost?"

"Not a ghost at all. I am very much alive. But I thought to find you with your vision restored."

The old man shook his head. "I could not bring myself to pray to Lord Buddha. Without you by my side, what difference if I live in darkness or sight? I came home to wait until I could join you in death."

"Oh, Father." Shim Chung's eyes brimmed with tears. They fell like a soft rain onto her father's face, moistening his cheeks and anointing his eyes. To her amazement, her father's eyes focused, unmistakably, upon her features.

"O my daughter, you are more beautiful than I had ever imagined."

Father and daughter rejoiced at the miracle. The king declared a holiday and invited all of his subjects to a feast. Everyone was able to eat their fill of delicious dumpling soup, delicately seasoned and stir-fried bellflowers, hearty mung bean pancakes, and sweet rice wine cake for dessert. At the end of the banquet, Lord Buddha chose to show his compassion and mercy. Every blind man, woman, or child who paid their respects to Shim Chung was blessed by the miracle of sight.

"Shim Chung the Lotus Queen" is a retelling of the classic Korean folktale "The Blind Man's Daughter." A favorite and well-known story in Korea, the tale of Shim Chung seems to be little known in America. Like much of Korean folklore, its main theme revolves around praising the virtue of young women who display great filial loyalty and piousness. It has also been translated into a ballet, which I wish I could've seen.

The Tears of My Mother, the Shell of My Father

I did not dwell overmuch upon destiny, living among the priests in Oda, sweeping the steps of the *jinja* shrine, and meditating at the seashore. Until the morning the Heikegani crab with the face of a samurai etched in its sepia armor came ashore and spoke to me.

As was my habit in those summer days, I had risen to greet the dawn. Hime, my white, four-legged shadow, tagged at my heels, more fascinated by the lapping waves than she ever was by a scampering mouse or the wings of a bird—a proclivity which ensured her welcome among the life- and peace-loving priests: a death-colored cat that never killed. Kneeling on the rocky beach that bordered the shrine, I faced the northeast expanse of endless waves. The first threads of silver brushed the horizon as fingers of water swept the shore. They curled into soft fists and retreated, leaving behind the crab.

It was large for its kind, its carapace as wide as my outstretched palm. Hime curled her tail around her paws as it scuttled from the water, her golden eyes impassive. I envied her composure. The crab approached with far greater alacrity than the dawn's warmth, and I scrambled from my posture of meditation.

It did not menace me, but rather tilted its shell so I was treated to the visage of the scowling samurai on its back. I had never credited the stories that linked these creatures to the ghosts of the Taira who died in the Battle of Dan-no-ura—although I was scrupulous never to eat their meat—but never before had the shell formations seemed so lifelike.

The flat eyes blinked open, transforming from the hard curve of burnished almond to the liquid and living orbs of a man. They fixed upon me, and the shell-sculpted lips rippled apart.

"Boy, I did not die so you could languish among the priests, contemplating rocks and trees."

The crab used the high speech of the courts in the manner of a lord to an inferior. I was so astonished that I did not think to be offended.

"Honorable, er, crab, I apologize if I have somehow wronged you—" I began.

The carapace-face scowled. "To think my son would grow to be such a simpering weakling. It took a fearsome *oni* demon to finish me, and your mother fought like a tigress that you might live."

I gaped at the crab. "Son?"

The face's expression softened. "Perhaps it is the priests I should blame. Nevertheless, the time for indolence is over. In three days it will be the anniversary of our murders. If you would honor we who bore you, go to your mother and staunch her tears."

"M–my mother?" I had never known the comfort of a mother. I had been surrendered as a squalling infant to the kindly, albeit reserved, care of the priests.

"They hewed off her feet so she could not run. Now she stands on Mount Mori, telling her tale to all. Free her and avenge me before the sun dawns on the fourth day, or I will curse you as a faithless son."

The crab swiveled and marched back into the dappled waters. As we conversed, the dawn had transformed into morning. Adorned with glittering jewels of sunlight, the sea crested over the samurai's helm, erasing dimension, color, and expression from the drab shell. In a spray of brine, the crab sank into the depths and was gone.

I stared for long moments where I had last seen the animated visage of a father I had never known. Hime groomed a creamy paw as though nothing had transpired more momentous than sunrise. She miaoed, and it shook me from my stupor.

I pelted back to the shrine, leaving Hime to complete her feline ablutions.

Kannushi Akihiko was making offerings to the kami as I burst into the *jinja's* heart. Although I all but danced with impatience, he continued pouring a trickle of *omiki*, ritually purified sake, into a pottery dish, before turning to acknowledge me.

He bowed, and with belated decorum, I returned the courtesy.

"Hiroki-kun," he said, "I see from your sandals that you did not choose to wade in the tide pools this morning. Were they not as enticing as yesterday's?"

Remorse suffused my face. In my agitation, I had blundered into this sacred space without removing my footwear.

"Sensei, forgive me." I wobbled, balancing on one leg as I struggled to undo the laces of my *waraji*.

He padded past me in immaculate socks, his feet silent over the shrine's floor. I hopped after him, one sandal dangling from my hand and the other still affixed to my foot.

"A crab spoke to me," I blurted as he paused at the shoe cupboard to retrieve his own *waraji*.

He seated himself on the entranceway's raised ledge to better don his sandals. "What did it say?"

Akihiko was my favorite priest. Although the eldest of the brotherhood—his face creased and seamed as ancient parchment—he was the only one who would tie up the hem of his robes to splash in the sea with a young boy and who always had time to hear me with a solemn face and boundless patience, whether I was complaining about the prevalence of pickled eel at dinnertime or musing about the nature of the infinite. But now I wished he would register disbelief to better match my turmoil.

"It said it was my father's spirit. It told me it would curse me if I did not comfort my mother who cries without feet on the mountain. But that's ridiculous, isn't it? It was a Heikegani crab, and surely I'm not descended from the Taira clan."

Waraji neatly affixed, Akihiko rose and strolled outside. I hobbled after him, admonishing myself for my single-shoed predicament—both for taking off the one and forgetting to replace it when I had the opportunity.

In the shadowed canopy of a copse of elm trees, Akihiko settled into an attitude of serenity. I plunked myself beside him and hurriedly laced on my detached *waraji*.

"Why are you so certain that you cannot be Taira?" he asked. "Have you had so many encounters with talking crabs that you have determined they are prone to uttering falsehoods?"

"B–but, I can't be nobly born. I'm nobody of consequence."

"You are as you have always been. The circumstances of your birth cannot grant or detract consequence."

"But—"

"Your given name is Taira no Chikazane. Your father was Taira no Sukemori, the second son of Taira no Shigemori, who was the first son and heir of Taira no Kiyomori, directly descended from Emperor Kuammu himself."

Each of his words penetrated like icy raindrops. "Why have you never told me of my heritage?"

"Would you have me send you into the world with only a single sandal?" Akihiko tapped my newly donned *waraji*. "As you have demonstrated, all actions must occur in their proper sequence. Omitting or neglecting any of the prescribed elements results in shame, imbalance, and disharmony." My sock, visible as it protruded over the straw toe, was begrimed from my clumsy pursuit from shrine to copse.

"My family's honor is more than a mishap of footwear!"

"Exactly."

I waved my hand, seeking to dispel the cloud of confusion Akihiko's words had created. "The crab said my mother wept on the mountainside. But it also said they were both murdered."

"A perplexing riddle. I have found that the best means of unraveling an enigma is by meditation. Truth typically reveals itself once one has achieved enough clarity to perceive it."

He closed his eyes.

"Sensei, I can't just sit here and meditate. I must go to Mount Mori."

"As you will, Hiroki-kun. But do bring along your book of sutras and a calligraphy brush so you may continue your studies. I also recommend you take a jar of *omiki*. Sake is so refreshing after a long trek." His hand dipped into his sleeve and pulled out a slender porcelain container. "How convenient that I poured an extra jar this morning."

I accepted the rice wine, bemused and exasperated. "Thank you, Sensei."

He cracked an eye open. "And put on clean socks before you go."

It seemed foolish to collect those things Akihiko had suggested, pointless delay. If I had not been in the habit of obeying him, I would have marched myself off without hesitation. In frenzied haste I retrieved brush and book and donned a clean pair of socks. As I pulled them on, Hime appeared.

"I must go off to perform the duty my father

commanded," I told her. "But don't worry. I'm sure the priests will fill your bowl with fish and rice every day."

Duly outfitted, I set off for the torii, the shrine's physical and metaphysical gate. However, I discovered that Hime had no intention of letting me embark alone upon my mission. She sidled at my legs, ignoring my efforts to shoo her—both cajoling and scolding alike. Reasoning with a cat is as futile as arguing with the waves, and rather than waste more time, I gave up. Thus, Hime padded beside me as I ascended that grandfather spirit steeped in age and grandeur, Mount Mori.

We trekked the slender trail while the sun slipped from the eastern gates and wheeled across the palace of sky. As the sun retreated into her western pavilion, I cleared the debris from a ditch, our shelter for the night. It occurred to me—belly rumbling and teeth chattering—that in my hurry, I had neglected to provision myself with so much as a rice ball or tinder box.

Hime did not immediately chastise me for my blunder. First she miaoed politely, inquiring after supper. But when I showed her the emptiness of my sleeves, her cries turned plaintive.

"Forgive me, gentle one. Tonight, you and I must go hungry. But as soon as it's dawn, I will look for a stream to fish. Come, curl up in my arms; at least I can endeavor to warm you."

Hime fixed me with her golden eyes and, quick as only a cat can, bounded away. I debated for a heartbeat whether I should let her go and trust her to return. But Hime was a pampered creature, unfamiliar with wilderness dangers. I would never forgive myself if she came to harm.

I chased after. Fortunately, a white cat's coat is well suited to catching stray beams of moonlight, and I glimpsed her stalking through the underbrush.

"Hime-chan, come here," I called. But, in the infuriating manner of catkind, she allowed me to approach only close enough to tantalize before leaping away. She led me a merry chase, crashing through prickly scrub and wending through dense foliage. At last, I saw her crouched atop a boulder. Around her perch, a stream rippled, mirror-bright.

With detached amusement, Hime let me pluck her from her roost. I had every intention of scolding her, but the notion fled when I saw the woman standing in the stream.

She was beautiful, her inky hair flowing in a mantle down her back. Her kimono was embroidered brocade patterned with elegant butterflies. But where her legs should be were trailing wisps of nothing. Tears coursed from her empty eyes, mingling with the smoke and mist of her absent legs, to join with the scrolling stream.

"Come closer," she whispered, "so you may hear my tale."

I did not move, only clutched Hime tighter. "Noble lady, I can hear you well enough from here."

"Then listen. When the *oni* came, my husband bade me run so that I and our son might live. But it was to death I fled. Treachery and assassins, they spilled my life on this stone. My last sight was of a black-garbed killer turning to slay my baby. Husband and child murdered. I am doomed to an eternity of sorrow."

I swallowed. "Who was your husband?"

"The noble samurai, Taira no Sukemori."

"Then you need no longer mourn for your son. He was given to priests to be raised and is in good health, notwithstanding an empty belly."

"Liar! For shame, to taunt a grieving mother. Your disrespect has earned you a *yurei*'s curse!"

"Would you damn the son you gave your life to save?"

The *yurei* of my mother studied me, still weeping black tears. "Prove you are he, and I will depart for the Pure Land and give you my blessing instead."

"What proof would you credit?"

"Only the reverence a son owes the memory of his mother." She clasped her hands in the sleeves of her kimono and waited.

The reverence a son owes the memory of his mother? Unnerved by the *yurei*'s wet, unblinking stare, I contemplated the boulder. Such an ominous rock, not like the sacred stones that adorned the shrine's provinces. The thought of my mother's spirit anchored here, chained by violence and tragedy, weighted my heart. Maybe I could not free her, and perhaps she would curse me for my presumption, but I would be comforted, knowing that the boulder, at least, had been honorably consecrated.

I had not taken priestly vows yet, but I had attended many purification ceremonies, and thanks to Akihiko, I had a jar of *omiki*. And did not the priests say that a single, sincere prayer could move heaven?

I tore several empty pages from my sutra book, ripped and folded them into lightning-shaped *shide* streamers, and bound them with grass to the handle of my calligraphy brush to craft a makeshift *shide* wand. Bowing to the world's corners, I strove for tranquility.

"Heavenly kami and earthly kami," I intoned, "hear me." My hands trembled as I flicked the *shide* wand over the boulder. "Purity of Heaven, purity of Earth, sweep impurities from within and without." The *shide* rustled and shushed, a familiar sound, holy and restful. "I beseech the kami to cleanse and bless this place so my mother may know peace." I bowed and unstoppered the jar of *omiki*. My hands no longer shook as I poured the sake onto the boulder. "Reverently, I speak this prayer. *Kashikomi kashikomi mo maosu.*"

When I was done, my mother's *yurei* raised her head to the starry sky. Her eyes were bright as hope, and she no longer wept.

"Surely, only a dutiful son would forgo food and drink to bring *omiki* to honor the place of his mother's death," she murmured. "I am content. What will you do now, Chikazane-kun?"

"My father's spirit called upon me to avenge him. I must kill the *oni* that murdered him."

A tiny crease appeared on my mother's brow. "It is the hasty hunter who lunges for the rustling bush before he knows what it conceals." She bowed. "Or the hungry one. At least I can keep your clamoring belly from clouding your caution. But beware that your true quarry does not elude you as you chase after a paper tiger."

I opened my mouth, abuzz with questions, but a bubble of light whirled from the heavens, stealing away breath, words, and opportunity. It whispered around my mother, playing with the hem of her kimono as it bore her aloft. She glanced back, and the expression on her face was both tender and pensive.

"Chikazane-kun, follow the stream up the mountain," she called, "and you will find the oni's cave and perhaps the steel beneath the paper."

Then she was gone.

Where she had been, a ball of flame danced on the water. It glided across the surface and settled atop the newly sanctified boulder. While I gaped, it flared bright as fifty lanterns, and before I could raise a hand to shield my dazzled eyes, it shrank to a comforting blaze. At the base of the boulder, a sumptuous banquet had materialized: roasted fish, steamed rice, and plum wine.

Enticed by the aroma, Hime bounded to the feast. A well-mannered cat, she awaited my attendance before commencing her meal, but she made her impatience clear by the anxious lash of her tail.

I was not so amazed as to require Hime to wait longer; I hurried to join her.

The fish was delicious, each mouthful a harmony of subtle flavors and delicate textures. The rice was perfectly cooked, neither too sticky nor too dry, and the plum wine was refinement itself. As we ate, the flame imparted an atmosphere of cheery hospitality and restful warmth. Despite having no fuel but the stone at its base, it seemed capable of burning indefinitely. At the completion of our meal, lulled by a sated belly, the cozy fire, and Hime purring at my side, I slept.

My dreams were filled with terrifying images of blue-skinned demons, barbed fangs glittering as they lunged at me. The murky gauze of dawn brushing my eyelids was a welcome reprieve.

Although the fire still burned, merry and warm, I shivered, chilled by my nightmares. Roused by my agitation, Hime opened her eyes and yawned.

"Ah, Hime, it is all good and well for my father's spirit to exhort me to confront an *oni,* but I do not even possess a katana." I stood, and Hime grudgingly rose to her paws. "Not that I could wield one. And this *oni* defeated my father, a mighty samurai. How am I to keep from being devoured, much less avenge him?"

"Master, please forgive this one's presumption, but neither *Kannushi* Akihiko nor your mother's spirit held any delusions as to your fighting prowess, even if the crab was inclined to bluster." The voice was soft and fluid as a purr.

I cast about, but there was only Hime.

"The priest, in his eminent wisdom, provisioned you with *omiki,* which you applied to masterful effect."

Incredulous, I watched her feline mouth shape words.

"It is this one's humble estimation that master is adequately equipped for this undertaking, although perhaps— and I mean no disrespect—it would have been advantageous to have brought an extra fishcake or two."

"You can talk!" I blurted.

Hime regarded me with unblinking, golden eyes. "You have conversed with your father's spirit manifested upon a crab shell and consoled the *yurei* of your mother, and it is *my* speech you cannot credit?"

"B–but you're a cat!"

She gave her back to me, the twitch of her ear showing her affront.

"Hime-chan, I meant no discourtesy. I am only amazed. Why have you never spoken before?" But she would not relent, and I was left to apologize to her stiff tail.

She stalked upstream, leaving me to tag after. The morning passed in stilted silence. As the sun crested overhead, I fetched out my book of sutras in a bid to win her forbearance and flipped through it.

"How could priestly meditations help me defeat an *oni*?" I mused aloud.

Hime glanced over one white shoulder. "So now you have decided to heed the words of a mere cat?"

"Hime-chan, if I have offended you, then I am the basest of villains. We have been fast friends all my life, and assuredly you have my most earnest confidence and trust."

A tentative purr rose from her throat, but her tail remained implacable.

"Surely you are the wisest and cleverest of cats, and it is my sincerest desire that you help ease the burden of my loutish ignorance. Please, Hime-chan?"

Her tail relented. "Hannya-Shin-Kyo," she miaoed.

I paged to the appropriate sutra. "Meditation upon emptiness of form?"

"It is not merely the emptiness of your mind that it brings about, master. Does not *Kannushi* Akihiko say that to embrace the sutra, you must become it?"

"Yes, but I don't see—"

"Exactly." Hime sat so abruptly I almost trod on her tail.

"Why have you stopped?"

"Shh! The *oni's* cave is around that bend. I scent the old death of discarded bones, and his *youki*, his demon energy, prickles my whiskers."

I froze, my heart leaping in my chest.

"He breathes deep and slow," Hime whispered, "as a bear in torpor."

"Then now would be the time to strike. If I had a large stone or a tree branch, perhaps I could—"

Hime flattened her ears and hissed. "Are you in such haste to be devoured?"

"What? I—"

"If you truly trust me to look after your best interests, remove your clothes and give me your calligraphy brush."

As I was not at all in a hurry to be eaten or rent to bits, I did as Hime instructed, although more than a little abashed at finding myself unclad at the dictates of a cat. I hid my garments in the long grass and detached the *shide* streamers from my brush, cringing at each crackle and whish.

Hime bade me lay the book on the ground opened to Hannya-Shin-Kyo. Rising to her hind legs, she took the brush in her paws and used the stream's water to moisten my ink stone.

She wielded the calligraphy brush with dexterity, her claws and paw pads daintily manipulating the slender instrument. Starting at my feet, and referring often to the book, she painted the sutra on my skin. I kneeled and lay supine so she could continue decorating my flesh, shifting when she requested so she could paint my back. The brush whisked, damp and prickly, from the top of my scalp, including the ticklish curve of my ears, to the space between each toe.

"There," she said at last. "Your flesh has become Hannya-Shin-Kyo."

The novelty of the situation had eroded when I lay facedown in the dirt. "And how is this to benefit me against the *oni*?"

"You must discipline your mind to match your body, and you will be to the *oni* as the silence that frames a heartbeat, the stillness between thoughts, and the space outside the borders of the poet's composition."

"How do you know this?"

"I am a cat."

She said it as though it was all the answer I should require, and perhaps it was. After all, who was more adept than a cat at lurking unseen and gliding upon noiseless paws?

I composed myself, although the *oni's* proximity was not conducive to serenity, and strove to attain that elusive quietude where heart and mind embrace emptiness and the path of enlightenment becomes clear. I closed my eyes, pushing aside thoughts of the *oni,* my duty, and even the grit beneath my naked skin. I chanted the Hannya-Shin-Kyo and found a corner of tranquility.

"An estimable accomplishment, master," Hime said. "I can no longer see you. But linger a while. Horses approach."

I heard the jingle of leather and metal and the thut-thut of hooves.

"I must warn these travelers away from the *oni's* den," I murmured.

Hime did not reply.

"Hime-chan?" I stood, and she did not stir an ear tip, only continued to gaze at my previous posture.

Wonder would have sundered my tranquility, so I let it drift past, unmoved as the mountain by a breeze.

The horsemen drew closer, a trio of men. At their head rode a nobleman garbed in the elegant uniform of a military lord of high rank. The train of his ocean-blue brocade spilled off his horse's haunches. The silk was embroidered in white and silver threads with graceful butterflies identical to the ones that had adorned my mother's kimono—the Taira crest. *My* crest. The soldiers beside him wore simple gray, blazoned with the shogun crest of Minamoto no Yoritomo. Taira and Minamoto, implacable adversaries riding in accord?

I chased after as they cantered around the bend. In the side of the mountain, a black mouth dribbled water from a stony throat. The three men dismounted and tied their steeds away from the cave's entrance. The Taira nobleman strode forward.

"Oni!" he bellowed. "Rouse your lazy bones!" His voice bounced among the rocks, the echoes lingering.

A thunderous howl blasted from the darkness, and I clung to the nothing of Hannya-Shin-Kyo, setting each syllable like a shield against terror.

Out of the cave, a monstrous figure emerged, as tall as two men and massive as four. Its skin was the blue of smoke, and black horns sprouted from its head. A ragged tiger pelt draped its hips, and a gnarled, iron club, thick as my waist, hung from a ginger-striped thong.

"Who dares?" it roared.

The nobleman pulled a tawny jewel from his sleeve. It drank in the sun and cast off brilliant streamers of light. "Bow before me, demon, or feel the *gofu's* bite."

The *oni* crashed to its craggy knees and kowtowed.

I almost lost the rhythm of Hannya-Shin-Kyo then. The jewel, the *gofu*, was the pivot upon which my destiny revolved.

"Forgive me, master." The *oni's* voice was harsh, the grate of bone upon rock. "I forgot the cadence of your speech in the passage of seasons. What is your bidding?"

"Did you also forget the date? Tomorrow marks the end of our compact."

"I know the date." I felt the *oni's* words rumble through the hollows of my chest.

"And tomorrow will herald the beginning of a new one."

The *oni* snarled, baring a mouthful of jagged teeth. "No! You promised to free me."

The nobleman sneered. "So you may split my skull and devour me? I think not."

"I am oath-bound to exact no retribution upon you."

"I am not so foolish as to trust the pledge of a demon."

The hatred in the *oni's* eyes was as plain as it was tangible, hot as the blast from a furnace and black as deceit. "It seems that I am the fool to have credited the words of a traitor."

The nobleman brandished the jewel. "Malign me again, and I will set the *gofu* in burning coals and watch you writhe while your insides smolder."

"You may hold the key to my *youki*, Taira no Kimitake, but if you forswear your vow, the safeguards of our pact are forfeit. One day, I will rend the meat from your bones and feast upon your screams."

Kimitake laughed. "Empty words, barren threats. While I possess the *gofu*, you must serve me faithfully."

The *oni* spat. "With so much duplicity blighting your ki, how long do you think your good fortune will last? My patience is boundless."

"I, not the uncaring infinite, govern my fortune."

"Indeed."

"Enough of your insolence. I have decided that it is time again for my fortune to rise. The empire is tranquil, and so the emperor looks fondly upon Yoritomo. Therefore, I command you to upset this inopportune peace. Tomorrow you will raze the shrine below and slaughter all within it. While the countryside stews in turmoil, I will challenge and defeat you, and the emperor will set me as shogun in Yoritomo's place."

"You would defile a sacred place?"

"Of course not. But you would."

The *oni* glared in impotent fury as Kimitake and his escort withdrew.

As evening's cloak swept over the mountainside, Kimitake and his men organized a camp—raising a tent, gathering wood, and cooking rice. Kimitake retired while his soldiers paced the perimeter.

I crept into Kimitake's tent, secure in the protection of Hannya-Shin-Kyo, although I deemed it wise to wait until both guards' backs were turned and Kimitake's snores were loud and even before I scrambled in.

While I had expected to rifle through the sleeves and folds of his uniform, or perhaps upend boxes and baskets in search of a secreted compartment, the *gofu* was plain to see. Kimitake's outflung arm revealed a hand enveloped in a skein of white silk. Layer upon layer of fabric, sheer as a butterfly's wing, wrapped the *gofu* tight against his palm. By the wan flame of the single, burning lamp, it glowed through the bindings like a star.

Another item I had not provisioned myself with: a knife. But then, I had emptiness of form, better than any blade. I hoped. Murmuring my sutra, I began the onerous chore of unknotting and unwinding the silk. Before long, I knelt in a pool of air-light whiteness. But as I tugged the final strip, I felt sweat tickling my forehead. Without thinking, I rubbed it away. My fingers came back smeared with black, the Hannya-Shin-Kyo characters smudged from the droplet of perspiration.

Kimitake's eyes started open. We shared a moment of fright, then he flung himself away, gripping the *gofu* in both hands.

"Guards!" he shouted.

The two soldiers barreled in, knocking me to the ground. One thumped my head with his fist, while the other drew his katana.

"Wait!" Kimitake called.

The speeding katana stopped, its tip a child's fingertip from my throat.

"Before you die, thief, tell me who procured your services. Who knows about the *gofu* and the *oni*?"

"My service is not procured," I said.

Kimitake ignored my denial. "Tell me who spies upon me at Yoritomo's court. Give me the name of the man who dares plot against me, and your death will be quick. Otherwise, I will ensure that your last hours are a banquet of suffering."

"I am not from Yoritomo. My name is Taira no Chikazane. My father was Taira no Sukemori."

A sinister smile curved Kimitake's lips. "Sukemori's brat. You survived, after all. No matter. The detail of your death was only postponed."

He displayed the *gofu*, taunting me with the gem under my chin. "Be cheered, boy. You will die as your father did."

I stared at him. "*You* are the steel beneath the paper."

Kimitake swept from the tent, gesturing to his soldiers to bring me. He snatched up a burning brand while they hefted me like a sack of rice and dragged me to the black cave mouth.

"Oni!" Kimitake shouted. "Come out. I have a gift for you."

The ground shivered as the demon emerged. "What is this?" he grumbled.

"Do you not recognize him?" Kimitake said. "You devoured his father many years ago. I would have spitted him upon a katana as a babe, but now he shall meet the same fate as Sukemori."

"He is only a boy."

"He is old enough to die. Sukemori's death was too easy. You will eat his son alive, beginning at his feet." Kimitake flaunted the *gofu*, shoving it at the *oni* like a weapon. "Obey me!"

Hissing and yowling, a milk-white star detached itself from the abyss of sky and sped through the air. It struck Kimitake's outstretched hand, and the *gofu* flew out, an arc of gold. Four red stripes crossed Kimitake's wrist, possibly the first blood that Hime had ever drawn.

For a heartbeat, we hovered, frozen. Then the *oni,* Kimitake, his two soldiers, and I scrambled after the *gofu.*

The torch dropped, sputtering and dying on the ground, and all was blackness. Around me, the sound of frantic movement swelled the night, accompanied by the *oni's* bellows. A man screamed, and I heard silk and other, thicker things torn asunder. The chime of drawn steel rang out.

I crouched in the dark, searching. It was an impossible task. I would never find the tiny jewel before the *oni* turned its fury to me.

"Hime, I can't see it!" I shouted.

"Clarity!" she yowled. "Heed Akihiko's wisdom. This is another truth."

It seemed a questionable time to meditate, but I did as Hime advised. I inhaled and pushed aside the wet, ugly sounds erupting in the darkness, exhaled, and let my terror leave with my breath. I whispered the syllables of Hannya-Shin-Kyo and embraced the stillness between thoughts like a warm robe against the cold.

In the quietude of my mind's eye, I saw the sun. It floated upon the horizon in glorious brilliance, wreathed in garlands of fire.

I plucked it from the sky and opened my eyes.

In my hand, the *gofu* blazed, turning the clearing from night to noon. All activity stopped, fixated by the radiant jewel.

The *oni* gripped his iron club in a monstrous claw. At his feet, both of Kimitake's men sprawled in unnatural poses, their blood soaking the ground. Kimitake had drawn his katana.

"Oni, stop!" I shouted.

The demon regarded me. "I have no argument with you, son of Taira no Sukemori. Give me the *gofu*, and I will not trouble you."

"Do not believe him!" Kimitake shouted. "He is a demon and lies as easily as he breathes."

"As you do." I stepped forward. "Oni, lay down your club."

The *oni* did not obey, but only stood, watching me.

"Fool!" Kimitake cried. "You think possession gives you mastery over a demon's *youki*? It took me years to learn the secrets of the *gofu*. Give it back, or the *oni* will kill us both."

"I think he will not harm me while I hold it. Is that so, oni?"

The *oni* rumbled assent. "But know, young Taira, that though you hold my fetters, I will not volunteer the key. I will not willingly embrace slavery."

"That demon killed your father," Kimitake said.

"You may as soon blame my iron club for Sukemori's death," the *oni* growled. "I was your tool."

"Unbound, it will destroy indiscriminately. Demons have no honor, only hunger and lust."

I faced *oni* and kinsman. "The demon has shown more honor than you." I flung the *gofu* at the *oni*. Fast as thought, the *oni* snatched it from the air. He popped it into his gaping mouth and swallowed.

"Fool!" Kimitake shrilled. He slashed at me, a killing stroke, and the world slowed. For the third time that night, I watched my death approach. But again it was deflected, this time by the bluntness of iron.

"No," the *oni* said. "You have harmed this one enough." A claw snaked out, taloned lightning, and seized Kimitake around the waist. The club came down on the nobleman's head. A slight tap, but it rendered Kimitake senseless.

The *oni* bowed to me, the man clutched in his fist like a limp doll. "Your father was an honorable man too. You should know that his dying request was that I spare his wife and son. I was taken by his sincerity. I could not save your mother, but it was by my intervention that Kimitake's assassins did not find you. And it was my envoy, pledged to secrecy, who saw you safely to the priests' care."

"Envoy?"

"Here," Hime miaoed, twining herself about my ankles. "Have I not taken good care of you?"

"Wondrous good care." I kneeled to stroke her white fur. Purring, she sprang into my arms.

"Should I be concerned at the intricacies of your machinations, oni?" I asked.

The *oni* chuckled. "If I were younger, perhaps. But the spinning of the universe is long, and I have shed enough blood this turning of it. I wish nothing more than to meditate upon enlightenment and be left alone." He grinned at Kimitake. "But first, I will have a fine meal."

Hime and I made haste down the mountain, not wishing to be privy to the *oni's* vengeance.

We paused only to fish the stream by my mother's boulder, and so passed beneath the torii's gate well fed and bearing a bounty of fresh trout. I remembered to doff my *waraji* before I strode into the shrine, and I bowed low to Akihiko as he poured an offering of *omiki*.

"Welcome back, Taira no Chikazane-dono," he said.

"You must always call me Hiroki-kun, Sensei. All that I am, I owe to your teachings. After I have taken my priest's vows, I will explore my destiny with the name Oda no Chikazane to honor both my parents and this shrine. But to you, I will be Hiroki."

Akihiko smiled and bowed.

As was our habit, the next morning, Hime and I rose to greet the dawn. But though we watched the whirling surf until the sun gilded the waves, not a single crab came ashore.

"The Tears of My Mother, the Shell of My Father" came about when Sean Wallace invited me to contribute a story to the anthology Japanese Dreams *from Prime Books. He also asked for some idea of what mythology my story would incorporate as he wanted to avoid contributors duplicating subject matter. What started out as an idea sparked by Lafcadio Hearn's "The Story Of Mimi-Nashi-Hoichi" (from* Kwaidan*) turned into a historical fantasy about the coming-of-age of Taira no Chikazane (aka Oda Chikazane) with a talking heikegani crab, a*

bakeneko, a yurei, and an oni. A bit nervous that Sean might think I'd gone overboard, I gave him the rundown. His response: "Yay!!"

Year of the Fox

In the lush countryside of the Middle Kingdom, a family of *huli jing*, fox spirits, hunted, danced, and barked their musical laughter. One night, as Master Sun turned his face away from the land and Mistress Moon drew a glittering veil of clouds and stars over herself, Mother Fox sat her children down to explain to them the way of enlightenment.

"Foxes are by nature a bit wicked," she said. "We delight in tricks and thefts, for our paws are silent and our minds quick. But it is one thing to charm a bird into one's jaws and quite another to revel only in mischief. For while we are greatly tempted, likewise great is our reward if we are virtuous."

Mei, the vixen cub, sat with one ear swiveled to Mother and the other distracted by a fearless moth. "Mama," she said, "what kind of reward? You mean a juicy rabbit or succulent egg?"

"No, no. A reward better than earthly delights."

Jin, the male cub, chewed at a burr caught between the pads of one paw. "What could be better than an egg?"

Mother barked, high and sharp. "Listen, my children, for you are almost grown! Enlightenment is your reward for being good foxes. It is the pathway into heaven whereupon we escape this wheel of mortality. Otherwise we are doomed to return again and again after we die, redressing the wrongs we have committed."

Mei leaped up, her jaws snapping shut around the moth. She licked her muzzle. "I'm hungry, Mama, when will we go hunting?"

Mother cuffed her. "Pay attention, cub. Have I ever taught you wrongly? Was it not I who showed you how to listen for mice tramping about underground?"

Mei sulked. "Yes, Mama."

"And was it not I who taught you to find crunchy beetles among the rotting logs?"

"Yes, Mama."

"So heed me."

"But my belly rumbles," Mei whined.

"You must learn to rule yourself, or you will never earn enlightenment."

"May we not earn enlightenment on full bellies?" Jin asked, rolling on his back to show that he was an obedient son.

Despite his display of respect, Mother growled. "Very well. I will bring something back to stuff in your greedy maws. But you must wait here so your clumsy paws do not prolong the chase."

Both cubs meekly bowed their heads.

Mistress Moon trod the arch of heaven, her veil sometimes modestly concealing her face and sometimes slipping shamelessly. The fox cubs, peeping from the entrance of their den, watched her erratic display unperturbed, for they knew she was inconstant and fickle. But she seemed particularly leisurely that night, dawdling to gossip with the celestial fires and flirting with the wind.

"Where is Mother?" Jin finally asked. "My belly is so empty I think it has started eating itself!"

Mei rose to her paws. "She has been gone too long. If we

wait much longer, I will surely die."

Without Mother's guiding nips and sharp eyes to curb them, the cubs grew giddy with freedom. They frisked beneath the stars, admiring how Mistress Moon turned their russet fur silver, and splashed in winking streams that trilled songs of adventure and secrets in the burbling language of *shui*, water.

Laughing, her tongue lolling to the side, Mei froze mid-bark, all four paws rigid in the earth. A familiar scent had darted past her nose—one of comfort, warmth, and home. It drew her, straight as hunger, to a still puddle of softness, hidden beneath a leering hedge.

"Jin, I found her! Mama, Mama, we've been looking for you!"

But Mother did not move. She did not yip a welcome, even when her cubs scampered to her side.

"Mama?"

She lay at a strange angle, most unnatural. Her neck bent backward, and the smell of blood was thick in the air. Mei nudged her with her nose. She saw in the moonlight a shining glint that encircled her throat. It cut through thick fur and flesh. Leaning close, she saw that Mother's back was broken, and most horrible of all, where her tail had been, proud and lush, there remained only a bloody stump.

Mei skittered back, rubbing her face in the cool earth, as though that would cleanse the sight from her mind. "We need to leave here. It is a place of death."

"What do you mean? Mother is asleep."

"She is dead. A fox hunter's trap ended her life, and a fox hunter's knife took her tail."

A trembling seized Jin from ears to paws. "Dead? No, she cannot be dead. Just this night she was lively and spry."

"Much can happen between twilight and dawn. Come away."

Jin began to cry, his howls piercing the night. Mei tilted her head back and joined him in his fox song of mourning.

Brother and sister lived together for a while in a shallow scrape, a burrow they had stolen from a family of rabbits after spreading panic and havoc through their community. There they plotted revenge with eyes that glowed yellow in the night.

"It is humans who killed her," Jin said, "a senseless, cruel death. They did not wish for her flesh to eat, but rather coveted her fine tail."

"Foxes may be wicked, but humans are evil," Mei agreed.

"I hate all of them. I will bring them down in their pride and folly. In the name of our mother, I swear it."

"I too," Mei said. "We will wreak madness and despair upon those who dare to think foxes may be conquered by cowardly snares!"

"I will turn myself into a handsome youth," said Jin, "and lure a holy monk from his sanctuary with cries for help. Then I will trick him with my magic into thinking a goat is holy. He will anoint it with precious oil and bow down before it. How I will laugh when I clear the magic from his eyes and he learns that he has been worshipping a foul goat!"

"That is nothing," Mei said. "I will turn into a beautiful maiden and make some unsuspecting man fall in love with me, or better yet, some unsuspecting lady. Think how dismayed they will be when I reveal my true fox shape!"

Jin bared his teeth in glee. "Such wonderful sport. We will prove ourselves to be the most cunning, the most sly foxes in all the Middle Kingdom. It will make our mother laugh as she watches from the lap of Buddha. Let us meet back here in a year to share the tales of our adventures."

Mei watched as her brother used *huli jing* glamour to shed his red-gold fur in lieu of a silk robe of malachite green with wide sleeves that swept the ground. Tawny streaks of embroidered lightning crisscrossed his back, outlined in gold and carmine threads. His face, without its fur, was still pointed, with a sharp chin and tapered ears. His eyes were wide and dark, as mysterious as the night sky, and they glowed, giving his fox nature away.

"Better avoid their torches," Mei said. "Or they will realize you are not one of them from the fire of your gaze."

Jin frowned, displeased that his disguise was less than perfect. "Aren't you going to change shape?"

"I will choose my form after I have stalked my prey," she said. "To better savor the joys of the hunt."

"As you will." Jin lifted his arm in farewell as Mei dashed away. "Remember, one year from today!"

Mei flicked her tail in acknowledgement.

<hr />

The maiden wore a coarse, roughly woven *shenyi*. Her name was Lian, which meant "graceful willow." Mei thought it was a most fitting name, for though her tunic was drab, brown hemp belted with a simple cord, and the skirt was tattered and threadbare, Lian might have been wearing the finest brocade. She moved as though she were a princess in the imperial palace, each step as lithe as a dancer's, with a calm serenity that rivaled a priest's.

She lived with two elderly servants, Chen and Ping, a man and woman so ancient the only indication of their sex was their attire. Whether sewing, cooking, or weaving, Lian went about the day's chores with a glad and merry heart. At night, when the lanterns blossomed to life, she read aloud from slender books of poetry and proverbs, or practiced calligraphy.

Mei watched her from a nest of bamboo in the forest that surrounded the mud and straw hut. When she hungered, she stalked mice and beetles, swallowing down the tiny sparks of their lives in a fierce snap of her jaws. Though Mistress Moon and her attendant stars tempted her to dance beneath them, she stayed still, not wishing to alert her quarry that *huli jing* lingered near.

A pure soul such as Lian was fine game. Foxfire visions to trouble her dreams would strip the tranquility from her mien, and barking demon shapes with dripping fangs that lunged and tore at her from the shadows would shatter her composure. Mei grinned.

One night, as the vixen contemplated the particulars of her strategy, she heard rustling in the bamboo forest. Curious, as all foxes are, she looked to see who approached.

The stench of the interloper assailed her delicate nose. He was unwashed and rank, smelling of night soil, fermented rice, and blood. Over his shoulder was a dingy sack with many rents in it, and in his hands, a curious curl of wood linked at the ends by sinew. A long fang lay upon the string. Mother Fox had taught her about human surrogate teeth so Mei understood its purpose, although she found the details of its operation perplexing.

She crept from her hiding place and joined herself to the man's shadow.

It was obvious this man was a villain, a bandit who preyed upon the unsuspecting. The vixen fretted. All her planning would go to naught if this man despoiled Lian in her stead. Still, the world was wide and full. Would it not be easier to find other prey to torment than to intervene?

While Mei vacillated, the bandit pushed open the hut's flimsy door. He drew upon the sinew with its long tooth until it sang with tension. At the movement, his sack shifted, and a portion of what it contained spilled out: a fox's tail.

This man was both a bandit and a fox hunter!

Mei barked in fury. At her outcry, she heard stirring within the hut. The man swung to Mei, his fang now pointed at her. But she had seen how he moved and was confident she was quicker. She leaped, sinking her teeth into his leg, and the next moment, his false tooth hurtled faster than Mei thought possible. It tore into her side. She had scarce moments for surprise before night slammed his fists closed around her.

As the world spun away, Mei wondered what Jin would do when she was not there at their appointed meeting.

Mei had not expected to open her eyes again, at least not in this world, perhaps on celestial Mount Tai where souls ascended after they died. So she was surprised to take in Lian's room. She lay on the maiden's bed, bundled in a straw blanket. She recognized the low table with its calligraphy brushes and the thin books stacked beside it.

Mei's side was wrapped with clean bandages and smelled of herbs and medicine. It pained her greatly. The blood flow had stopped and there was no scent of corruption from the wound, but she was weak as a newborn cub. She could barely swivel her ears.

She wasn't dead. Why?

As though in answer, Lian entered, pushing aside the ragged curtain. The maiden bowed when she saw Mei's eyes upon her. She held a bamboo tray upon which sat a bowl of clear water and a bowl of *congee*, rice porridge.

How, mused Mei, *could a creature with only two legs move with such grace?*

"Mistress Fox, I see you are awake. Please be at ease, exquisite one. You are not well and should lie still." Lian folded to her knees beside the bed. "You must be hungry and thirsty. There is a little fish in the porridge, and the water is fresh. It would do you good to eat and drink."

Lian set the bowl of *congee* under Mei's nose. The savor of clean, sweet rice and the delicate aroma of broiled fish made her mouth moist with yearning.

The maiden lifted a pair of chopsticks from the tray and

used them to offer Mei a ribbon of fish.

The vixen accepted the tidbit. It was delightful. Her belly clamored for her to gobble the whole bowl as fast as she might, but she had better manners. She let Lian feed her and forced herself to chew each mouthful slowly before swallowing. Between bites, Lian offered Mei sips of water from the bowl.

"You are a most mannerly fox," she said. "Chen and Ping said you would growl and snap, but I knew you would be courteous. After all, why would you save us from a bandit one moment and then bite off my hand the next?"

Mei was strangely reluctant to disillusion Lian of her courtly fox notions, so she accepted the water without baring her fangs, and she let Lian run her fingers through her coat. And when the maiden cuddled Mei in her arms, soothing away fever and cold with the comfort of her body, Mei did not even contemplate nipping her.

One night, when the moon was a sickle of silver shining against the darkness, Mei waited for Lian's breath to slow in the deepness of Lord Sleep's realm. Her wound no longer troubled her, and she was shamed she had allowed herself to fall into the care of her enemy. She ran from the hut on secret paws and hid herself in a thicket of bamboo.

That night, Mei plied the stuff of spirit glamour, taking upon herself the shape of a noble lady. She gazed with pleasure upon the smooth skin of her white hands, delicate as nesting doves. A *pien-fu* took the place of her lustrous fur. Its loose folds of crimson wrapped her body, secured with a rippling, pink sash. The tunic of silk spilled to her knees, and the matching skirt was modest, long enough to conceal her tiny feet. A tasteful pattern of storm clouds adorned the cloth, embroidered with cream threads, highlighted in damson.

Conjuring false tears as easily as her false shape, she stumbled to Lian's doorstep.

She beat at the flimsy barrier and called piteously, "Help me, oh, help me! Won't someone have mercy on me?"

Immediately, Mei was rewarded by the sound of commotion from within. Lian herself swung open the door, and Mei dropped to her knees. She let the curtain of her glossy, jet-black hair fall so it covered her face.

With fox-born artistry, she allowed Lian to spy the liquid gleam of her eyes through the cascading strands of darkness. From such mysterious gazes, Mei knew, were human hearts beguiled.

"Oh, kind mistress," she wailed. "My escort was ambushed by a band of rogues. They killed my servants, and I had to flee for my life. I have been lost in the forest. Please help me!"

Without waiting for Lian to reply, for she knew the maiden would never turn such a pitiful traveler away, Mei crumpled in a pile at her feet.

"Chen, Ping!" Lian summoned her servants to help her carry the swooning lady inside. They arrayed Mei on Lian's bed (a familiar establishment for the vixen), and Chen and Ping fluttered about, brewing tea and lighting incense.

Lian dabbed cool water on Mei's wrists and forehead. When Mei sensed her bending near, she opened her eyes.

"Beautiful maiden," she whispered, "you are my savior. I am forever in your debt." Mei bridged the tiny space between them and pressed her lips to Lian's.

The girl pulled away in surprise.

Mei hid her face in the voluminous folds of her sleeve. "Did I offend you?" She peeked one eye out and was pleased to see Lian's face was soft with wonder.

"It was only—unexpected. You are safe now, mistress. Please do not be afraid. Although there are evil men about, we are smiled upon by good fortune."

"Do evil men come here often?" Mei pretended to quail behind her sleeve.

"Not at all. In the many years I have lived here, a bandit has only threatened once."

"What happened?"

"A fox protected us."

"A fox?"

"Indeed. She barked and bit the rogue. While he reeled about with her jaws upon him, I hit him on the head with a saucepan."

A saucepan? Mei pushed aside the laughter that threatened to bubble from her chest. "You are so brave. I feel so feeble beside you."

"You are a refined orchid, mistress. The notion of bandits sullying you with their stinking presence makes me wish I might have more than a saucepan to fight them with."

Mei flung herself into Lian's arms. "You mustn't call me 'mistress.' You are as a sister to me. Call me Mei."

Lian clasped the vixen close. "I am Lian, Mei, and I have always longed for a sister."

In the following days, as she lay ostensibly sick and wan, Mei found ways to display glimpses of her white flesh to her hostess: an ankle slipped from beneath her hem, the alluring shadow of her breasts covered by thin silk. At these exhibits, Lian always discreetly lowered her eyes, but Mei knew she had fascinated her. She spied Lian many times gazing rapt beneath the fan of her eyelashes.

"My sister," Mei said one day, "why do you insist upon sleeping on that thin straw mat on the floor? I know I have usurped your bed, but surely you do not think me so corpulent that we cannot share it?"

Lian laughed. "You are as slender as a young beech tree!"

After that, maiden and vixen slept in the virgin-narrow softness of Lian's bed. It reminded Mei of how Lian had warmed her in her arms when she had shivered with fever in her fox shape. But after all, if it hadn't been for Lian, she would not have been hurt in the first place.

She plied the maiden with tender kisses as she slept,

teasing desire from her like water from ice. Mei fed upon her sighs, feasting on stolen ardor, mounting desire, and passion. As the nights passed, Lian soon found excuses to linger by Mei's side, letting chores go undone where before she had always been diligent. She even set aside her poetry and calligraphy, preferring to sit and gaze upon Mei's beauty.

Time passed, dancing the seasonal steps of darkness and light. Every night, Mei drank a nectar of energy and passion from Lian's lips and curled herself into the warmth of the maiden's body. When the days began to trip over themselves in haste and the nights to lumber along like lazy donkeys, Mei grew bored enough to toy with Lian's brushes and riffle through her books.

"Where did you learn to read and write, my sister?" Mei asked.

"My family is descended from a revered heritage of poets. Hard times plundered the wealth we had, but as long as I have my books and my ink stone, I am still rich."

"I wish I could understand the characters you paint," Mei sighed.

"You cannot read?"

Mei shook her head, oddly bashful. "My mother never taught me."

"Would you like to learn?"

"Could I?"

So Lian demonstrated the correct way to grind ink and hold a brush. She taught Mei the characters for the five elements, *jin*, *mu*, *shui*, *huo*, and *tu*, and the character for soul, *ling hun*.

"You know so much," Mei said. "You belong in elegant palaces, not out here where there is only dirt and rocks."

"I have seen the inside of palaces. When my family was high in the regard of the emperor, I walked on jade tile and wore ivory combs in my hair. But when the fates and some politicians conspired to dishonor my family name, I found I did not miss those things." She tapped the spine of one of her books.

"Learning is a treasure that follows its owner," she quoted.

"But what of the glorious gardens and fountains?"

Lian laughed. "A book is like a garden one may carry in one's pocket."

"And the men who plotted against you?"

A look drifted over Lian's face, bringing distance and a hint of clouds to her eyes. "The Buddha extols us to forget injuries and remember only kindness. Who am I to rail at the wheels of fate? Perhaps I wronged them in a previous life and they are only righting the balance." Lian winked, the far-off look erased. "Or perhaps I shall redress what has happened in another life."

"You are a follower of Buddha?" Mei asked. "My mother once tried to instruct me on his wisdom, but I was impatient with her lectures."

Lian put down her brush. "I am not a monk or a wise man, but I know Buddha taught that what we undergo in this life is a result of our previous actions. Nothing is permanent in this world, and it is a place of suffering. But if we live as best we can, one day we will achieve bliss and end our time on the eternal cycle of rebirth."

That night, as the stars gazed in the darkness upon the Earth, Mei could not sleep. Her thoughts were jagged, fierce things, troubling her with their sharpness.

Was Mama's death due to the inherent evil of humans, or was it merely a turning of the karmic wheel? What if Mama, in a previous life, had wronged the fox hunter, and so it was mete she die in his wire? How then could it be virtuous to wreak havoc upon all humans in the name of vengeance?

Because foxes are natural liars, it was easy for Mei to tell herself falsehoods. But also, because of her natural affinity with lies, it did not take long before she scented her own pretense and knew it for what it was. More than the nature of enlightenment, the very thought of harming Lian pained her worse than any thorn in her paw or burr in her coat. She could no more contemplate undertaking her planned mischief than she could will herself another tail.

Embracing this truth was like a foretaste of enlightenment to the troubled vixen. It freed her from her restlessness, and she fell away into a chasm of dreams.

When the new dawn spread garlands of light through the hut, Mei found herself watching Lian with new eyes, ones opened by newfound tenderness. And with them, she saw something she had not noticed before.

"When did you become so thin?" she exclaimed.

Lian's cheeks, once as bright as spring peaches, were sunken. The maiden was pale, and her eyes seemed too large for her face.

"It does not matter," Lian replied. "For I rejoice that you grow stronger every day."

It was true. Mei felt more vigorous than she had ever been. She realized with rising horror she was so energized because of what she had taken from Lian. In the night when she plied the girl with secret touches and kisses, the delicious flavor she tasted was nothing less than Lian's ch'i, her vital energy.

At once, Mei vowed to stop her nightly caresses.

But despite her best intentions, Lian continued to fade. With sorrow heavy in her breast, Mei realized she must leave or risk irreversible harm upon one that had only shown her kindness and generosity. Only the power of time and the incisions of distance would sever the connection between their energies.

That morning, while Lian listlessly toyed with her breakfast *congee*, Mei hid her face in the shadow of her hair. "My sister, I think it is time our paths divided."

She heard Lian inhale, a gasp of distress. "Y–you wish to leave me?"

The vixen could not bring herself to meet the maiden's eyes. "It occurs to me that I have dishonored my family by evading my nuptial responsibilities. I may no longer face my ancestors if I do not return to my duty."

"But what of the bandits? And the nights grow cold. You must wait out the winter here, at least."

Mei's eyes burned with anguish, but she only shook her head. "I will embrace my fate, as I should have months before. Tomorrow I will set out."

"Tomorrow is too soon!" Lian's voice was ragged with distress. But no matter how she pleaded, Mei would not change her mind.

The fox maiden rose early to find Lian's shadowed eyes upon her. They did not speak while Mei dressed, nor when Lian bundled a rice cake into Mei's pink sash.

Outside, in the pre-dawn chill, they stood, not touching, avoiding each other's gaze.

"Be well, my sister," Mei said at last.

"May Buddha guide your steps," Lian whispered in reply. She burst into tears and fled inside.

Mei stood for many seconds before the hut's door, warring with herself. At last, she turned and walked into the forest. Buddha said that suffering was caused by craving. If she did not crave Lian, then neither of them would suffer.

When she had traveled a hundred paces, Mei shed her human form. Her fox body felt uncomfortable to her, stiff and unwieldy. It was strange to run on four paws, and she grew confused and giddy at the wealth of scents that beset her nose. She had spent so long as a woman she had all but forgotten what it was to be a vixen. And yet, she swiftly learned to once again savor the feel of the breeze in her whiskers and revel in the splendor of her tail as it furled in a banner behind her. It was, after all, high time she walked the ways of a fox once more.

Mei worked to clear her mind, embracing the fullness of delight which was paws upon the earth, night song in her ears, and the breath of sky through her fur. She meditated upon the shape of trees without their covering of leaves and upon the fragility of snowflakes as they drifted from the heavens. And when the winter frost grew bitter and food scarce, she accepted the chill of her limbs and her hollow gut with philosophic grace.

The crack-crack of the thawing river occurred in the completeness of time, and new-green buds dotted the skeletal trees. With a full belly once more, Mei contemplated the warm skies and delicate blossoms of spring with wonder.

Then one night, she heard a tendril of fox song in the darkness. She recognized the voice, though it was deeper and stronger since the last time she had heard it. A year had waxed and waned; Jin had returned.

Atop the hillock where they had romped as cubs, sister and brother met with joyful yelps and yips. Jin had grown, his slender body wiry and quick. In the year's passage, he had shed the last of his cub uncertainty; he blazed with vitality.

"Your voice thrills my ears," Jin said. "My eyes delight in your image!"

"Nose meets nose with happiness," Mei cried.

With the jubilation of their first greeting behind them, Jin sat, curling his tail around his haunches. "Now tell me, my sister, a year has passed. What magnificent trickery have you wrought?"

Mei flicked her ear, suddenly coy. "I am certain your adventures are more worthy of exultation."

"I hardly know where to begin. Why, more monks, priests, and magistrates than I have pads on my paws have been brought low by my cleverness. And the maidens I have dishonored! I suspect there will be many half-fox children before long."

Mei found it difficult to maintain her pretense of enthusiasm. "Oh?"

"But before I tell you of all my adventures, let us hunt together, as we did as cubs."

"Are you hungry?"

Jin barked in laughter. "Yes, for mischief! As I journeyed to our appointed assignation, I saw a virtuous maiden who lives with her elderly servants. She is called 'Graceful Willow.' Think how exciting it will be to corrupt her and bring her low."

"I do not think—that is—"

"What is the matter, sister? Such recreation so nearby and you hesitate?"

"I have come to the belief that it is better to eschew wickedness," she admitted.

"So it is true."

Mei was startled to hear the rage in Jin's voice. His molten eyes seethed with suppressed anger.

"The birds gossip and the trees whisper of the foolish fox who loves a human," Jin growled. "It could not be my Mei, I told myself, for we have vowed havoc upon all humankind. No sister of mine could be so treacherous as to dishonor the memory of our mother."

Mei trembled but only said: "A clear conscience does not fear devils at the door." It was a proverb from Lian's books.

Jin snarled. "Silence! I must clear this smear upon our family honor."

Mei cowered, tucking her tail low between her legs. "What do you mean?"

"I will attend to this human who has corrupted you. When I am through with her, you will be free of her."

"No! You will not harm Lian. I forbid it."

Jin screamed in rage, a high-pitched shriek that ripped the night. In a blur of claws and fangs, he launched himself at his sister and pinned her beneath his weight.

"Shameful bitch," he growled. "You dare to forbid me? You who have broken the oath we made."

"It was a cub oath," Mei whined, "made in haste and ignorance."

Faster than she could blink, Jin bit her tail, his keen teeth

pollen from its wings. Poised against the silk of her skin, it was like an iridescent jewel of onyx and topaz.

"Justice is a sword that must be wielded with thought and compassion, not impulse," she said. She raised her arm, and the bee hummed away.

"You are as wise as you are lovely," Hou Yi said. "Might I have the gift of your name?"

"I am Chang'er."

"And may I also continue to enjoy the radiance of your company?"

Chang'er lowered her eyes and smiled. "You may."

The Jade Emperor favored Hou Yi above all others, so when the couple came to him to ask for his blessing to marry, he gave it gladly.

Hou Yi and Chang'er wed in a magnificent celebration. They strolled along a star-strewn path, their feet treading golden clouds while silver roses and blushing orchids rained down. They shared the emperor's table, enjoying lotus seeds and honeyed dates with the imperial children, and drinking rice wine so light and pure, it was clearer than water and sweeter than cream.

After the banquet, the emperor and the Queen Mother swept aside the clouds so the whole court might be entertained by the bustle and commotion of the Middle Kingdom below. Both Chang'er and Hou Yi were delighted with the people who flourished in the land beneath the sky. Chang'er clapped her hands with pleasure when she saw how clever they were, writing poems upon paper and composing wonderful songs to honor their ancestors. Hou Yi gazed with fascination upon the farmers and fishermen who worked so hard to feed and clothe their families, admiring their diligence and good will.

But the nine sons of the emperor, being young and

impetuous, were not impressed.

"How dreary they are," the youngest said. "Look at me instead. I can shine like the sun!" And so saying, he leaped into the sky, bright as fire and ten times as hot.

Not to be outdone, his eight brothers jumped after him in a searing conflagration, flashing and burning with glee.

Hou Yi gaped in awe at the dazzling exhibit overhead, but Chang'er's attention was drawn to a lament from below. The terrible splendor of the emperor's sons had exacted a toll upon the Middle Kingdom. Rivers boiled away, crops charred and died, and people starved. A great cry rose up, imploring the Jade Emperor to bring an end to the punishing heat.

But the emperor only shrugged. "They are my sons, and they may do as they will." He gathered up the hems of his robes and turned his back upon the suffering below.

Chang'er wept as the people of the Middle Kingdom continued to wail.

"Please, divine princes," she pleaded, "end your sport before the land is scorched black."

But the nine sons were too enraptured by their own glory to heed her.

Chang'er turned to Hou Yi. "This is wickedness. My husband, you must do something. This cannot be allowed to continue."

Hou Yi was stirred by the distress in his bride's eyes. "Come down, sons of the Jade Emperor!" he shouted. "I will not ask you again!"

The princes jeered and flashed even brighter.

Hou Yi pursed his lips and took up his great horn bow. Nocking an arrow to the string, he took aim at the youngest. Even though the prince's radiance was blinding to behold, Hou Yi did not falter. He loosed the bolt, and it flew clean and true to the heart of the youngest prince. The imperial son plunged from the sky and fell, hissing and spitting, into the ocean.

The remaining sons, despite the loss of their youngest,

refused to desist. One after another, Hou Yi nocked arrows to his bow and shot the princes down.

When the Jade Emperor felt the furious heat ebb, he turned around and saw what had happened.

"You have extinguished my sacred heirs!" he cried. "For that, you and Chang'er shall die."

But his wife, the Queen Mother of the Western Heaven, intervened. "It is because of your pride that this has come to pass. You did not discipline your sons; therefore, I will not allow you to kill my handmaiden or her husband."

The Jade Emperor was still furious, but he acceded to the justice of his wife's words. He stripped away the immortality from archer and maiden, and flung them down to walk the Middle Kingdom, banishing them from the heavens.

The people of the Middle Kingdom were grateful to Hou Yi for saving them and crowned him as their emperor. Hou Yi dedicated himself to making wise decisions and aiding those in need. But he came to resent his subjects when he saw that even the diligent workmen could be subject to greed and pride— taking advantage of those poorer than they or reveling in drunken excess when there was yet work undone. He realized that the denizens of the Middle Kingdom could be as capricious as the rulers of the Celestial Palace, and as fickle. Chang'er witnessed the same follies as her husband, but instead of taking exception to the vices of mortals, she pitied them and continued to take pleasure in the beauty and wondrous creations they produced.

As the seasons passed, lines began to crease Hou Yi's face. His joints, once supple and strong, creaked and ached. One morning, he woke to discover a shining, white hair on his pillow.

"Alas, how ignominious it is to be defeated by ruthless decay, when once I was immune to death." He frowned into his mirror, cataloging and lamenting the symptoms of mortality he found in it.

When his advisors came to consult him on that day's

calendar, he shouted at them, "It is your fault that I will die!"

When the magistrates arrived, seeking his wisdom, he railed at them, "It is because of you that I will become a frail old man!"

And when the peasants began queuing up to petition his imperial judgment, he roared at them, "You have condemned me to the ravages of time!"

While his subjects glanced at one another in confusion, he screamed, "You must all repay me for my sacrifice!"

At his decree, the farmers and fishermen brought him the bounty of their labor, the magistrates piled silks and spices at his feet, and his advisors emptied the coffers in order to build a gold statue in his likeness. Due to this excess, children went hungry, and the people wore rags in their poverty.

Still, Hou Yi was not satisfied. "You must worship me, neglecting even your fields to honor me, for I have given up everything for you."

Chang'er withdrew into her garden as she watched her husband's rule become one of tyranny and madness. She retreated in silence, holding her tongue lest she worsen Hou Yi's temper with her unhappiness. Before long, she stopped talking altogether.

When Hou Yi could not coax a word from his wife, he flew into a great rage. He grabbed his bow and shouted up to the Celestial Palace, "If it is your will to banish me forever, then so be it. But your exile has stolen Chang'er's tongue. Give us a draft from the cup of eternal life, or I will shoot down the last sun!"

The Queen Mother of the Western Heavens heard him and flew down to the Middle Kingdom. "You would extinguish the life-giving warmth and plunge both the Middle Kingdom and the heavens into eternal darkness?"

Hou Yi set an arrow to the string. He pulled it to his ear and pointed it at the sky. "Restore our immortality, or I will create an endless night."

Seeing the wrath in Hou Yi's eyes, the Queen Mother mixed sacred herbs into a cup and poured a cool stream of time over them.

"There is enough elixir of life for you and Chang'er. Your wife, who has been guilty of nothing but compassion, may ascend to the Celestial Palace, but you can never return."

Hou Yi snatched the cup from the Queen Mother's hand. "So be it." He dashed with it to Chang'er where she sat in her garden, watching cherry blossoms flutter in the wind.

"Look," Hou Yi said. "I have tricked the Queen Mother of the Western Heaven into giving us the elixir of life. We never have to die, and I will rule the Middle Kingdom forever. I will shower you in jewels and drape your white limbs in the finest silk. Drink and speak once more."

Chang'er looked into her husband's face and saw only the fervor of his madness. Her heart ached in her breast when she thought of the ceaseless suffering the people would be condemned to with Hou Yi as their emperor. Her hands trembled as she took the cup he offered her. But they steadied when she threw back her head and gulped both her portion of immortality, and his, before he could stop her.

Tears like molten pearls coursed down her cheeks. "I'm sorry, my husband," she whispered. "I cannot allow you to be an eternal tyrant."

Hou Yi screamed in rage when he saw Chang'er had swallowed the whole draft. He leveled his bow and had an arrow nocked and pointed at her heart. But when he saw the grief in her eyes, he recoiled.

"I was about to shoot you," he cried. "What have I become?" Shame drove him to his knees, and with a deafening crack, he snapped his bow in half. Hou Yi reached his hand to his wife in entreaty. But though she stretched out her arms to embrace him in turn, they could not touch. Chang'er's feet drifted from the floor. Hou Yi was forced to watch, heartbroken and wretched, as she floated out a window and into the sky, pulled into the heavens by the potency of the double dose.

"I am immortal once more," she called, "so I may not remain in the Middle Kingdom with you. But I shall not fly back to the Celestial Palace. I will only go as far as the moon so that I may still hear your prayers."

As good as her word, Chang'er watched over the Middle Kingdom from her new home in the palace of the moon. She ensured that harvests were bountiful by watering the sky with her tears of loneliness. Hou Yi gazed up at her every night, never forgetting that because of his madness, they must be forever apart.

On the fifteenth day of the eighth month, the Queen Mother took pity on the parted lovers. She let Chang'er fly down to the Middle Kingdom and watched as the reunited lovers embraced.

The Queen Mother of the Western Heavens was so moved by the joy of the archer and her handmaiden that she gave Hou Yi a choice: "I will restore your immortality, but you must live on the sun and guard it from harm, in case another archer should decide to shoot it down."

"May I be with Chang'er?" Hou Yi asked.

"She chose the moon as her home. You may gaze upon each other in passing, but you may not meet. However, on this day, and for this day of every year, you may be together."

Hou Yi sank down in despair.

Chang'er knelt beside him. "One day is surely better than none, is it not?"

"I will live for that day and for the delight of seeing you again," Hou Yi said.

And ever since, Hou Yi and Chang'er are reunited on the fifteenth day of the eighth lunar month. On that date, couples often walk in the beautiful gardens of China and look up at the full moon where they know Chang'er gazes down upon them.

The traditional folktale of Chang'er, the Lady in the Moon, is a beloved one among Chinese people, who have a saying: "When the moon is full, mankind is one." One of a trio of moon legends that commemorate the Mid-Autumn Festival—a very important holiday on the Chinese calendar—it is second only to the Spring Festival (the Chinese New Year). To celebrate Chang'er and Hou Yi's annual reunion, people light paper lanterns, have picnics and parties beneath the round, harvest moon, and eat moon cakes—a dense, hockey puck-shaped pastry filled with sweet bean paste or mashed lotus seeds, nuts and dates, or sometimes a cooked egg yolk. I have a particular weakness for moon cakes and will, if given the opportunity, gorge myself silly on them.

Returning My Sister's Face

My earliest memories are of Oiwa in the sunlight, brushing her magnificent hair. Unbound, it trailed to the floor, a waterfall of shimmering black, the same color as a raven's wing. It was Oiwa who picked me up from the dirt with words of comfort and wisdom when my pony threw me off for shouting in his ear.

"Yasuo, do not cry, silly boy," she said as she dried my tears with the hem of her kimono. "And you should not rage at your pony either, but thank him for only tossing you from his back. If you had shouted in my ear like that, I would have bitten you besides."

And it was Oiwa's proud smile I looked for when I won the praise of my sword master. I remember how small she looked, kneeling in her kimono with her hands folded in her lap. But she was always my big sister, even when I towered over her in my samurai armor.

Our father died when I was a boy, felled by the sword of a barbarian from the west. He was a brave warlord. I barely remember him. Oiwa told me how he laughed when he swung me in his arms, proud of how fearless I was as a babe.

With his death, our prosperity ended. Mother grew sick, and people turned away from us, loathe to help those who had so obviously been touched by bad luck, as though it might be contagious. We would have become thieves or beggars if not for Shigekazu—the lord of Yotsuya. He took pity on us and took me in, gave me a swordsman's education, and let us stay in our ancestral home.

To repay him, when I earned my warrior's katana, I became his most loyal captain. I patrolled his borders and kept bandits from abusing his farmers and tradesman.

It was the start of plum blossom season during my seventeenth year when Iyemon arrived. The white and fuchsia petals shed their heavy perfume, and there was anticipation of the upcoming *Ume Matsuri* festival. Iyemon rode to Lord Shigekazu's gate, a masterless samurai, shining in his fine *michiyuki* overcoat, astride a golden stallion. He brought with him his katana and his servant, Kohei, and nothing else.

He went to Shigekazu and petitioned to be allowed to join his guard. In turn, my lord Shigekazu asked me to look after him.

It was strange for me, as Iyemon was a well-grown man, ten years my senior. Yet, I was in the teacher's position. Even so, Iyemon was gracious. He did not chafe when I instructed him as to how we set our watches and shifts, nor did he sneer to spar at bamboo canes with me. Indeed he laughed when I bested him in our first bout, and was as genial in triumph in our second.

He had no kin in the area and no hearth, so I invited him to dinner.

Oiwa was surprised to see three men—Iyemon, Kohei, and myself—walking up the path, but she was sweetly courteous, as I knew she would be. She ran to put more water on for tea and returned with a basin of scented water for us to splash upon our hands and faces.

If I try, I can still remember the flavors from that dinner. Hot soup with tangy seaweed, sticky rice that melted on my tongue, tart *umeboshi* from the plum trees, and sweet bean cakes that could have been clouds of nectar fallen from the heavens.

After the meal, Kohei washed the pots and bowls while Oiwa went to tend our mother. Iyemon and I sat on tatami mats and smoked pipes, awash in tranquil harmony.

With the blue smoke wreathing his face, Iyemon cast his eyes down. "Tell me, Yasuo," he said. "Why is your beautiful sister without a husband?"

I was surprised at how forthright he was on this matter of delicacy, but then he was new to Yotsuya and did not know our family's story.

"None will take her," I said. "For though Oiwa is noble, she can bring no dowry to a marriage. Our father died with his riches plundered. What household wealth we had we spent on medicine and doctors for our mother, who languishes with a wasting disease."

"But you have this fine house in the country—"

"We owe all to Lord Shigekazu. Without his mercy and generosity, we would be penniless, cast out into the streets."

"Still, your sister is sweet of face and graceful of temperament. Surely there are men who would take her to wife?"

"She is considered a bad luck woman," I admitted. "She has no suitors."

"Outrageous!" Iyemon declared. Of course, I was not going to disagree.

When Oiwa came from our mother's room, Iyemon rose to his feet and bowed low to her. A soft blush, like the new glow of camellia blossoms on a white bough, filled her face, and she hid behind her fan.

"Lady Oiwa," Iyemon said, "I would be honored if you would walk with me at the *Ume Matsuri* festival. May I call upon you tomorrow?"

My sister's blush deepened, turning the enchanting hue of sunset clouds at midsummer. "I will look forward to it."

The *Ume Matsuri* festival was the traditional start of spring. The plum trees displayed their five-petalled blooms during the month of *YaYohi*, while beneath them, maidens and youths strolled together. The maidens wore kimonos to rival the flowers—violet silk embroidered with golden bamboo shoots, apricot sleeves with scarlet chrysanthemum, sea foam brocade with glowing koi painted on them. And the young men wore the maidens like banners upon their arms.

Oiwa did not have much finery, as we had sold her most lavish kimonos long ago. But she had kept one kimono, our great-great-grandmother's good luck silk. It was peacock blue brocade with silver pine trees and malachite maple leaves woven through the cloth. With her hair piled high on her head and wooden geta sandals on her feet, Oiwa looked like a princess.

Iyemon's eyes widened when he saw her. He bore with him a perfect white plum blossom for her hair, and she let him affix it in her gleaming locks. They walked arm-and-arm together among the plum trees.

Iyemon became a frequent caller, and as the first cherry blossoms began to bud, they announced their *Yui-no* betrothal. Since there was but meager wealth on both sides, the gifts they exchanged were, of necessity, modest. Iyemon gave my sister a white obi to use as a belt on her wedding kimono. It was fine silk, embroidered with snow-white phoenixes. In return, Oiwa gave her husband-to-be a black *hakama* she had sewn with her own hands, every stitch a prayer of loyalty and fidelity.

At the wedding ceremony, Oiwa was radiant as the dawn star as she glided through the humble Shinto shrine of our ancestors. We had hired a maid from town to dress her hair with rented *kanzashi* combs and to help her don the traditional *shiro-maku* kimono.

Iyemon was composed, an expression of serenity on his face as he spoke the commitment vows. He looked like a king in his newly made *hakama* robe. Oiwa's hand was steady, without a whisper of tremor, when she lit the customary lamps.

But barely had the taste of the wedding sake faded when trouble visited. Our mother, too weak even to attend the ceremony, worsened. We thought death was ready to harvest her, yet she clung with grim tenacity to this world. The newlywed's month of sweetness was cut short, barely begun.

Then Lord Shigekazu received word that Lady Ami, his granddaughter, would be traveling from the city of Edo to visit him on her quest to find a husband. As he had not seen the daughter of his daughter in many years, he was jubilant at the news. He asked me to take a regiment of men to meet her at his border. For the first time, I was loathe to do his bidding.

"Please, Lord Shigekazu," I said. "My mother is very ill. I would prefer to stay near. Will you give me leave to decline this obligation?"

"Obligation?" Lord Shigekazu demanded. "Is it not basic courtesy that the captain I have raised as a grandson should feel honor-bound to protect the safety of my only granddaughter? What if there are bandits on the road? Come, Yasuo, your mother has had many a bad turn, surely she will last a fortnight longer?"

"Please, my lord, it is my least desire to defy you, but I also owe duty to she who bore me."

Lord Shigekazu might have said harsher words then, ones that would have made me lose face if I did not bow to his wishes, but Iyemon intervened.

"If my lord would be willing to indulge one so new to his service," he said. "I would be greatly privileged if I could take my brother's place as escort for the Lady Ami."

Lord Shigekazu's brow still creased with darkness, but he allowed the substitution as Iyemon was now my kin, and to refuse him would disgrace both of us. And so the next morning, Iyemon took his golden stallion and a regiment of my most trusted men to the Yotsuya borders.

There was a great storm that night. Rain clattered against the wooden shutters, and the fierce wind tipped and twirled the lanterns so their light cast stark shadows and dancing silhouettes. Oiwa and I kneeled by our mother's tatami mat, holding her hand and taking turns fanning her brow. She complained of a burning thirst, but her throat was too ragged to swallow the weak tea Oiwa brewed.

Mother's mind flitted like a bird between this world and the next. She rarely knew us, babbling instead as though we were spirits and ancestors long dead. I knew she would leave us soon. They say if someone sees their ancestors in a fever dream, it is not long before they will go to join them.

Oiwa continued to fight against the inexorable. "Mama," she whispered. "Mama, try to drink a little of this green tea. It will cool you."

Mother sat bolt upright and stared at Oiwa. "Where is your face?" she cried.

Oiwa reached a hand to her cheek. "I–It is at the front of my head, where it always is."

"No, only half of it," Mother replied. She glared at me. "I pledge you to return the other half of your sister's face. Swear it, Yasuo!"

Oiwa and I exchanged troubled looks. I do not swear oaths lightly, so I hesitated to promise to some fantasy of fever. But our mother was insistent.

"Swear it, or I will haunt you after I die! Swear!"

Oiwa leaned to me. "There is no harm in giving your word to something that requires no deed. Do not let her final words be a curse."

So I bowed my head over our mother's hand and promised to return Oiwa's missing half-face. I was uneasy, but truthfully, what harm was there in such a promise?

The next thunderbolt brought a sudden gale into the room, crashing open the shutter and blowing out the oil lamp. When we had relit it, our mother was gone, extinguished with the lamp, and unlike it, forever dark.

My sister's ragged sobs filled the room as she clutched

our mother's body to her breast. I bowed my head.

Lord Shigekazu's anger with me was somewhat assuaged by the news of Mother's death. Still, I knew he harbored resentment. After her cremation ceremony, he insisted I return to the soldier's barracks.

Though Oiwa was pale and weak with grief, she urged me to go.

"We must not lose Shigekazu's favor," she said. "We owe him a debt we will never be able to repay."

I knew in a mere fortnight Iyemon would return, so I packed my saddlebags and kissed her farewell.

I dined at home when I could escape for an evening so Oiwa would not be alone. She was always glad to see me, but grief haunted her eyes, and where once her cheeks were blushing peaches, they had begun to sink and grow sallow. I saw a strand of white in her lustrous hair, and it saddened me. Oiwa had spent her youth tending our mother. Now her joy had flown with Mother's death. I prayed that Iyemon's devoted attentions would be able to restore her joy, if not her youth.

As though in answer to my prayers, the gods delivered Iyemon at last. And like a sunrise, with him came the Lady Ami. Having spent time in the royal courts, she was like a jeweled butterfly among moths. She wore layers of fine, silk kimonos, twelve of them together, with the sleeve cuffs and collars cut to display each distinctive color—lilac, damson, azure, indigo, emerald, topaz, citrine, garnet, peach, scarlet, magenta, and finally at the last, creamy white—and each one embroidered with a different design in gold thread.

It seemed all the unmarried men in Yotsuya found themselves captivated by the flashing hems of Lady Ami's kimonos and the elusive perfume she wore—jasmine and crushed lily. I, along with half my men, wrote poems of love and admiration to her.

But then, more misfortune. Word came of raiders from the west, great men with shaggy faces and beastly apparel, plundering the countryside. I was assigned the duty of quashing their incursion before it became an invasion.

It was with a mournful heart that I left Lady Ami's presence, but I did not dare to protest. I was already low man.

The barbarians were vicious and tenacious. They had set up a rude fortification on the edge of Yotsuya. I knew if I did not disperse them, they would foray deeper in, burning villages and razing fertile farmlands. I organized my men for a siege.

The month of rice planting, *UTzuki*, passed, then the month of rice sprouting, *SaTsuki*. Summer lapsed in a blur of sun and waiting. My soldiers took turns fishing the waters and hunting the forest for our meals. We cooked upwind of the barbarians to torment them with the smell of fresh fish and sweet rice while they were reduced to hard loaves and dry meat.

It was my turn with net and rod. The water laved cool around my knees, and I grew lost in thoughts of the perfection of Lady Ami's face with its dusting of rice powder. A great tug on my line nearly pulled me over. I called my men to help bring in the grandfather fish.

We soon saw it was not a fish tangled in my line. It was a most terrible article I had caught—two bodies, nailed to either side of a black door, the prescribed punishment for convicted adulterers. They were purple and bloated. Her face in particular was most terrible to look upon. Half of it seemed to have melted away as though it were wax beside a fire.

I swept away the debris of riverweed from the grisly plank. The woman was wrapped in a peacock blue kimono, the silk ruined by the water. I could make out the memory of silver pine trees and dark green maple leaves outlined on the brocade.

It was Oiwa's festival kimono. O my sister! And sharing her door of disgrace was Iyemon's servant, Kohei. I recognized his face and the *yukata* robe he wore.

I do not know what I screamed then—a curse on my sister, or on the gods, or on myself. I bolted from that place, flung myself upon my stallion, and galloped away.

I rode through rain and sun and night until my steed collapsed beneath me. Then I ran. When my armor and helmet weighed me down, I tossed them aside. I kept only the clothes on my back and my katana, for I would need it to spill the cursed blood from my veins at the altar of my ancestors.

It was night when I stumbled through the gardens of my ancestral home and up the steps of our shrine. I ignited four sticks of incense and lit four candles, the number for death and misfortune. Around me, the icons of the most revered ancestors of my lineage—dukes and warlords and virtuous ladies— watched as I removed my soiled and tattered shirt. I felt their eyes as I knelt and drew my katana.

"Yasuo, do not cry, silly boy." Oiwa stood in the shadow of a bamboo screen, holding a fan over her face. I leaped to my feet, ready to embrace her. But when she came closer, I saw by the light of the four candles that Oiwa had no legs. Where in the darkness I had thought them concealed by night, in the circle of candleshine, I saw she trailed away to a wisp of translucence.

"Oiwa," I whispered, "what has befallen you?"

"Remember the oath you made to our mother?"

"Y–yes."

"I call upon you to honor it." She dropped her fan. What had been dreadful on her poor body, on her visage as a *yurei*, an angry ghost, was even more terrible. One side of her face was sweet and whole, the other melted away. One eye rolled in its socket, yellow and diseased. A crust of tears tracked from it down her sagging cheek. Her once-opulent hair was lank and thin, dirty strands hanging from her torn scalp. Half her mouth was curled down, black and putrid, a wad of spittle hovering at the edge. And the skin on that cheek and that side of her brow was gray and curdled.

I shrieked in horror, and there was only blackness.

I woke in the shrine, the four candles burned away, and the cloying scent of incense hovering in a cloud. Iyemon supported me, dragged me to my feet.

"I thought the voices in the garden were cats fighting or the shriek of night birds," he said. "If I had known you had returned, my brother, I would have run to your side."

"I was fishing," I mumbled, on the edge of delirium. "There was a door. Oiwa and Kohei." I remembered terrible images of Oiwa, her face dripping and her blackened mouth, but no, that was how I saw her on the door, surely?

"That is not how I would have had you learn of it. Come inside. I will tell the sorry tale."

Within, Iyemon poured me a bowl of plum wine which I drank in two gulps. He poured another that I clutched in trembling fingers.

"It was my fault," Iyemon said. "If I had not volunteered to escort Lady Ami to her grandfather's house, perhaps Oiwa would not have gone mad with loneliness."

"What are you saying?"

"I found them together. Oiwa drank poison, some mixture of the garden—suicide. I treated Kohei to the blade of my katana."

"My sister was an honorable woman!"

"I would not have revealed their sin, truly, but—"

"Liar!" I shrieked. "Get out of my house!"

His face, so beseeching a moment before, hardened. "Yasuo, this is now *my* house. Your mother bequeathed it to Oiwa, and as her husband, I am her beneficiary."

The half-full bowl of wine shattered on the floor. "You

are throwing me out?"

Immediately, he was the picture of solicitude. "No, no. Never. I do not blame you for your sister's wantonness. But you must face the truth."

I sank to my knees, sobbing like a child, calling to Oiwa. Iyemon left me alone to preserve what little honor I could still lay claim to.

In the subsequent days, I refused to leave the house, and Iyemon let me brood and weep as I would. He also left me casks of plum wine and bags of opium to ease my grief. Welcoming the blunting of memory, I drank and smoked my days away.

It was during one of these opium-muddled twilights that Oiwa returned.

The peacock blue silk of her kimono was stained by river water, but she protected me from the worst of her terrible appearance. She held a paper fan across the sinister half of her face.

"My face is still half missing," she said.

I scrambled away, cowering in a corner of the room. "What face do you want to recover?" I whimpered. "Your honor or your beauty?"

"Ah, little brother, you have come to the crux of it. Know this, while you have sunk yourself in wine and opium, the nuptial plans rush forward. I will return on their wedding night. Look for me then. See to it my face is restored that night, or I will haunt you forever."

"Oiwa, I'm so sorry."

Her voice softened. "Do not cry, little brother. I have shed enough tears for us both."

Then she was gone, and all the opium cobwebs swept from my mind with her.

It was dark, the sun long fled beneath the horizon. I crept from my chambers, disheveled and bleary. Voices drifted from the sitting room, two men at dinner. I clung to the shadows and listened.

"It was a fortuitous day when you came to Yotsuya." It was Lord Shigekazu.

"I am honored that you say it, my lord," Iyemon replied.

"Come now, surely you can call me 'grandfather'?"

"I would not wish for unseemly haste."

"Tut. Your *Yui-no* to my granddaughter can be announced soon enough. It is well you discovered your wife, that slattern's betrayal, and dealt with her and your servant so decisively. Otherwise the smear on your reputation—"

I did not breathe while I struggled to make sense of their words. Shigekazu as Iyemon's *grandfather*? Iyemon engaged to Lady Ami?

It was the first revelation. The second came after their words penetrated further. Shigekazu had said *dealt with her*, meaning Oiwa. Iyemon had told me my sister had taken poison—dishonorable suicide. But now it seemed more likely Iyemon had dispatched her himself.

A lie. It is well known that falsehoods come in threes. This was the second lie, the first being that Oiwa had been unfaithful. But the third lie I did not yet know.

I slunk back to my chambers. While I poured the last of the wine onto the thirsty rocks outside (for I did not wish to be tempted by the seduction of euphoric forgetfulness), I mused over the question. I was about to scatter the opium to the winds when I paused.

I put on fresh clothing—a short *haori* jacket and *hakama* pants—as befitting a lowly servant. Stealing Iyemon's golden stallion from the stable, I rode to Lord Shigekazu's pavilion. There, I slipped through the watch corridors and guard niches I knew so well from my time as Shigekazu's captain, until I came to Lady Ami's chambers.

By the light of a muted lamp, I set a porcelain plate by her head and set fire to the opium until a deep, sweet smoke filled the room. In order to keep my own head clear, I wrapped my face with the silk sleeve of one of Ami's kimonos. It also muffled my mouth and thereby my voice, which further served my purposes.

When I was sure she was deep in the opium's thrall, I spoke.

"Ami, Ami," I intoned. "This is your ancestral kami, your family's spirit of fertility. If you wish to bear sons, you must honor me."

Ami mumbled and stirred.

"Speak up, Ami, I cannot hear you," I sang.

"What do you want?" Her speech was sluggish. "Let me sleep."

"If you wish for your union to Iyemon to be blessed with sons, you must answer my questions so I can cast your horoscope."

This seemed to pique her interest. "How many sons will I have?" she murmured.

"As many sons as the fortnights of your courtship."

"That is good. We will have many sons."

"Was your courtship so long?"

She laughed, her throat sultry. "He courted me as soon as he saw me on my palfrey, on the very border of Yotsuya."

"As your escort?"

"Even then."

"Was he not married?"

"I suppose so, but it is common knowledge in the emperor's court that wives are but a passing inconvenience."

Such a place of depravity the emperor's house must be. "Did you plot with Iyemon to loosen this 'inconvenience'?"

"A noblewoman does not dirty herself with such details. But when his wife and his servant were found forming the double-backed demon, well, I was hardly surprised."

It was enough. I had discovered the third lie. It was Ami herself. Where Oiwa had been pure and innocent, Ami was corrupt and evil. My fingers trembled to wrap around her traitorous throat. I loomed over her, but then I felt an icy touch at my shoulder.

I glanced back, almost upsetting the lamp when I saw Oiwa's *yurei*. Thankfully, she continued to shield her face with her fan, although her single clear eye was baleful.

"In order to bear sons," she said, in imitation of my kami voice, "you must marry Iyemon tomorrow."

"We have only just announced our intention to marry to Grandfather today."

"Regardless, you must marry tomorrow or you will be barren forever."

I stared at Oiwa. What was she about?

"Do you understand me, Ami?" she demanded. "You must marry tomorrow!"

"I will, kami. I will."

"Do not forget." This last she directed at me, but Ami, with her eyes shut, did not notice the difference.

Oiwa's fan fluttered, an unspoken threat, and she dissolved into the night.

Trembling like a wind-wracked pine tree, I smothered the still-smoldering opium and blew it cool before pouring ashes and plate into the pocket of my *haori* jacket. I made sure to light incense to mask the scent as I skulked out of Ami's room. Making as much haste as I dared, I darted to where I had stashed Iyemon's stallion and rode him full out, all the way back.

I had him re-stabled, my clean clothes shucked, and the ashes of the opium smeared in my hair while Iyemon and Shigekazu lingered over sake. After Shigekazu returned to his pavilion, Iyemon came to my quarters with a jar of wine, which I dutifully drank.

The next morning, Iyemon trotted me out. A man from the town came to shave and dress us. Through this purification, Iyemon continued to ply me with wine. I drank enough to keep my hand steady and my resolve strong, but poured two bowls out for every one I drank.

Iyemon dressed in the black *hakama* Oiwa had given him, a travesty of my sister's devotion.

"Why the finery?" I asked, speaking the words as though through half-numbed lips.

"I am to become engaged to the Lady Ami," Iyemon replied. "As you are my brother, I think you should know before the public announcement. I would prefer to stay single, for my heart lies yet with Oiwa, but Lord Shigekazu insisted. He thought good fortune could be restored to his house by a prosperous match."

The lies tripped so easily off his tongue. "I don't begrudge you happiness, my brother." I giggled like a courtesan, high-pitched and merry, and pretended not to see the look of disgust on my "brother's" face.

When the guests arrived, I played the drunkard for them all, spilling tea and sake, and tripping over my own feet.

Shigekazu, especially, was revolted by me. After I groped one of Ami's maidens, he grabbed me and dragged me from the house. It was what I had hoped he would do.

Dropping my dissembling act, I bowed low.

"My lord, I hope you will forgive my display. I needed to speak to you in private."

He was surprised at my sudden lucid speech, but he was not inclined to hear me. He twisted away.

"Wait! My ancestors have warned me. They have given me two things to share with you. If you recognize the signs, will you humor me?"

He turned back, suspicion and distaste marking lines in his brow.

I handed him the plate from his granddaughter's room.

"Why, this is the expensive plate I gave Ami when she arrived. How did you—?"

"Lady Ami will insist that the wedding be held today," I

said. "She will not be swayed. This, too, my ancestors divulged to me. Will you hear me?"

"If Ami insists upon marrying Iyemon today, which I know she will not, then yes, I will."

How Shigekazu's eyes bulged when Ami announced she wished to go to the temple that very day to wed Iyemon. No words could change her mind, and so their *Yui-no* engagement became their wedding party.

And that is how I pressed lord Shigekazu into accompanying me in hiding behind a bamboo screen in their wedding chambers. His patience with me was at its limits, though. It was the height of impropriety for us to be there, but when the bride in her *tsuno kakushi* veil stepped into the room, her face concealed, he was as silent as I could have wished.

Behind her, Iyemon followed, and together they lit the ceremonial lamps.

"Why such haste, my blossom?" Iyemon said. "It goes against the plan we made and looks improper."

"Do you not burn for me after all, my husband?" Through the veil, Ami's voice was muffled and strange. My blood turned chill and slow. It was not Ami's voice at all. I had heard that cadence, that tone every day as a boy, singing and talking and shouting. I would know it in my sleep. It was Oiwa.

My plan had been to force a confession from Iyemon and Ami at blade-point, witnessed by Shigekazu. My sister's *yurei* had other intentions.

Iyemon wrapped his arms around his bride. "How could you ask such a thing?"

"I just wonder if you truly wished to marry me. Were your words of promise lies? Did you instead plan to stay with your wife, Oiwa?"

"Oiwa? That bad luck slut?" Iyemon stepped back. "How

could you think that?"

"Perhaps you did not intend for Oiwa to betray you and were put out by it?"

He caught one of her lily hands. "Come, if it will make you believe my love for you, I will tell you the truth of Oiwa's fate.

"Oiwa did not betray me. She was utterly devoted to me, the simpering cow. You were jealous of her face, you said. She was so sickly after the death of her mother; it was easy to pour poison into her tea. I did it while she watched, calling it medicine. She took it from my hands with such trust. Didn't you hear how the poison I chose disfigured her? Would I have delivered such a caustic potion to anyone I loved?"

"Tell me the symptoms of the poison." Her voice turned harsh. Could Iyemon not hear it?

"It made her ugly, for your enjoyment, my love. It made her hair fall out in great clumps."

The figure of Ami reached under the *tsuno kakushi* and shed a handful of long, black hair with dried blood at their roots.

"What else?"

"Ami, what—?"

"What else!"

"H–her face, one eye grew swollen and infected, weeping pus and tears, while the skin puckered, rotting from within."

"She must have been in great pain."

"She screamed for hours."

Lord Shigekazu looked like the gods themselves had touched him, and they had used a heavy hand.

"It must have felt like a lifetime of suffering," the bride continued.

"Better her lifetime than mine. Come, let us lie together, my beautiful blossom."

He lifted his hands to the *tsuno kakushi*. The thin, white silk slid to the floor. Beneath it, as I had known, was not Ami's pretty face, but Oiwa's terrible one. The white rice powder did not conceal the crust of seeping yellow that oozed from her eye. Nor did it cover the bleak decay of her skin as it sloughed off.

"Come, my husband, kiss me." Oiwa held her arms out to Iyemon. "Embrace me."

Iyemon shrieked and pulled his katana from its sheath. With a single slice, he swept the head off her shoulders. It rolled to where Shigekazu and I spied from behind the bamboo screen.

But it was not Oiwa's face on that severed head, but Ami's.

Shigekazu and I scrambled from cover, away from the grisly remains. Iyemon screamed when he saw us, a cry of rage and madness. He charged at us with his katana upraised. I freed my blade, parried aside his wild strike, and Shigekazu tangled his legs from behind. I knocked his katana from his hand, and together, Shigekazu and I bound him. He gibbered all the while, raving that he saw Oiwa's face in the lantern, her *yurei* in the corner, her shadow behind the bamboo screen. When I glanced at these places, all I saw were lantern, corner, and screen.

Shigekazu sent for the magistrate and told them the whole story, clearing Oiwa of any sin. The magistrate sentenced Iyemon to death for his crimes.

In the days before his execution, Iyemon continued to screech and wail in his tiny cell, mad with terror. His eyes rolled in his head, following unseen specters, unknown horrors, all with Oiwa's face. In the end, the headman's sword was a mercy.

That night, I prayed before the altar of my ancestors.

"Oiwa, my part in restoring your honor is done. Are you pleased?"

There was no sound but the wind.

I did not see her again that night, or any other. Although I have heard stories in the village of a beautiful maiden wearing a peacock blue kimono, walking among the plum trees, singing. They say her face is exquisite, but her song sad.

"Returning My Sister's Face" is a retelling of the traditional Japanese ghost story "Tōkaidō Yotsuya Kaidan" (The Ghost Story of Tokaido Yotsuya) written during the Edo period by playwright Tsuruya Nanboku. It is one of the most famous ghost stories in Japan, reputed to be based on a pair of actual murders, and it has been adapted into dozens of movies, television dramas, and plays. Japanese actors believe they must pray at Oiwa's grave to receive her blessing before any production of "Tōkaidō Yotsuya Kaidan" or risk her wrath, much like speaking the title of "The Scottish Play" is taboo among Shakespearean actors. Actors are a superstitious lot, nothing at all like writers who are rational, reasonable, and sane. Macbeth Macbeth Macbeth.

Um, I need to go spit over my left shoulder now. "Fair thoughts and happy hours attend on you."

About the Author

Eugie Foster calls home a mildly haunted, fey-infested house in metro Atlanta that she shares with her husband, Matthew, and her pet skunk, Hobkin. After receiving her master's degree in Psychology, she retired from academia and became a corporate computer drone. When her company asked her to leave the phantoms and fairies in the South and return to the dead-cold lands of the Midwest, she said "no" and retreated to her library to pen flights of fancy.

Eugie's fiction has been translated into Greek, Hungarian, Polish, and French; received the Phobos Award; and been nominated for the British Fantasy, Bram Stoker, and Pushcart awards. Her publication credits number over 100 and include stories in *Realms of Fantasy*, *Interzone*, *Cricket*, *Cicada*, *Fantasy Magazine*, *Orson Scott Card's InterGalactic Medicine Show*, *Jim Baen's Universe*, and anthologies *Best New Fantasy* (Prime Books), *Heroes in Training* (DAW Books), *Magic in the Mirrorstone* (Mirrorstone Books), and *Best New Romantic Fantasy 2* (Juno Books).

Visit her online at www.EugieFoster.com.

Copyright and Publication History

"Daughter of Bótù" © 2008 by Eugie Foster. Originally published in *Realms of Fantasy*, Sovereign Media, August 2008.

"The Tiger Fortune Princess" © 2005 by Eugie Foster. Originally published in *Paradox*, Paradox Publications, Summer 2005.

"A Thread of Silk" © 2008 by Eugie Foster. Originally published in *Jim Baen's Universe*, Baen Publishing Enterprises, June 2008.

"The Snow Woman's Daughter" © 2007 by Eugie Foster. Originally published in *Cricket*, Carus Publishing Company, February 2007.

"The Tanuki-Kettle" © 2007 by Eugie Foster. Originally published in *Cricket*, Carus Publishing Company, July 2007.

"Honor is a Game Mortals Play" © 2007 by Eugie Foster. Originally published in *Heroes in Training*, Martin H. Greenberg and Jim C. Hines, eds., (Tekno Books) DAW Books, September 2007.

"The Raven's Brocade" © 2007 by Eugie Foster. Originally published in *Cricket*, Carus Publishing Company, December 2007.

"Shim Chung the Lotus Queen" © 2006 by Eugie Foster. Originally published in *GrendelSong*, Autumn Equinox 2006.

"The Tears of My Mother, the Shell of My Father" © 2009 by Eugie Foster. Original to this collection.

"Year of the Fox" © 2007 by Eugie Foster. Originally published in *So Fey: Queer Fairy Fiction*, Steve Berman, ed., The Haworth Positronic Press, 2007.

"The Archer of the Sun and the Lady of the Moon" © 2006 by Eugie Foster. Originally published in *Paradox*, Paradox Publications, Summer 2006.

"Returning My Sister's Face" © 2004 by Eugie Foster. Originally published in *Realms of Fantasy*, Sovereign Media, February 2005.

Printed in the United States
138983LV00002B/40/P

9 781607 620105